Zoey's hands wouldn't stop shaking.

Her heart was pounding so hard, it felt like it was going to burst through her chest at any moment. She saw Josiah's kayak sweep over the small waterfall and get stuck underwater. She climbed up the rock above, trying to keep Josiah's flailing body and boat in sight.

She pulled the fast rope from the bag on her hip. The timing of her throw had to be perfect. She pitched the rope toward Josiah with all her might. The line uncoiled as it flew in Josiah's direction. It landed near him, within a foot or two. But Zoey knew that he was probably getting disoriented from the total onslaught of the water.

"Josiah, grab the rope!" she shouted.

The water was churning, making visibility difficult. And there was no telltale tug, no sign at all that Josiah had seized the cable...

Kathleen Tailer is a senior attorney II who works for the Supreme Court of Florida in the office of the state courts administrator. She graduated from Florida State University College of Law after earning her BA from the University of New Mexico. She and her husband have eight children, five of whom they adopted from the state of Florida. She enjoys photography and playing drums on the worship team at Calvary Chapel in Thomasville, Georgia.

Books by Kathleen Tailer

Love Inspired Suspense

Visit the Author Profile page at LoveInspired.com.

ALASKAN WILDERNESS MURDER

KATHLEEN TAILER

LOVE INSPIRED SUSPENSE
INSPIRATIONAL ROMANCE

LOVE INSPIRED® SUSPENSE
INSPIRATIONAL ROMANCE

Recycling programs
for this product may
not exist in your area.

ISBN-13: 978-1-335-58773-2

Alaskan Wilderness Murder

Copyright © 2023 by Kathleen Tailer

For questions and comments about the quality of this book, please contact us at CustomerService@Harlequin.com.

Love Inspired
22 Adelaide St. West, 41st Floor
Toronto, Ontario M5H 4E3, Canada
www.LoveInspired.com

Printed in U.S.A.

I will lift up mine eyes unto the hills, from whence cometh my help. My help cometh from the Lord, which made heaven and earth.
—*Psalms* 121: 1-2

This book is dedicated to Zoey Garner
and all my other young readers. May God bless you
as you pursue the life and plans God has for you!

It is also written in memory of my precious son,
Joshua Evan Tailer, who died at the age of twenty-three
on April 23, 2022. We miss you terribly,
but will see you soon in Christ!

ONE

She was drowning.

Large pockets of air had already been expelled from Zoey Kirk's tortured lungs, and the pain was excruciating.

She needed oxygen, now!

Panic swelled within her. The instinct to try to breathe underwater was strong, but she fought it with every ounce of strength she had. She knew as soon as the icy water filled her lungs, it was the beginning of the end, but she was in sheer agony as she ran out of oxygen. She couldn't even call for help. Pain radiated across her chest and shot down her arms and legs. The icy water surrounding her sent spears of anguish along her eyes and nose. There was a roaring in her ears that sounded like a giant freight train coming straight for her. She struggled to touch the ocean's surface, which seemed only inches away, but every time she got close, she felt hands pressing down against her head and shoulders, making her stay just beneath the surface.

Although it was hard to think of anything but sheer survival, on some level, she struggled to understand what was happening. The last thing she remembered was seeing the iceberg calve and sink into the ocean, sending waves shooting out in all directions. She had quickly taken stock of the location of each of the ten kayakers she was leading and had glimpsed Mia Phillips's kayak in trouble as she was overcome by the crest of a wave. The woman's kayak had capsized, throwing Mia overboard. Thankfully, Mia had followed the directions Zoey had given everyone on this expedition—if you have a problem, stay with your boat and signal for help. Zoey had reached Mia in two short minutes and then jumped into the water and swam underneath Mia's boat. A couple of quick shoves and the kayak had easily turned back over in one smooth motion. Then she had steadied the paddle craft as she'd helped Mia get back in. As she had tried to get back into her own kayak, however, something hard had hit her head and she had landed back in the water herself. Had she bumped against the boat or a paddle? She couldn't remember. Her brain seemed fuzzy, and nothing else mattered but getting oxygen into her lungs.

Still thrashing in the icy cold water, Zoey felt someone reaching for the clips on the front of her life vest. Was somebody trying to take off her vest to ensure she drowned? It was unthinkable. She struck out wildly against the hands and arms that were assaulting her but still couldn't positively identify her aggressor. Surely Mia wasn't trying to hurt her. Had someone else approached? There had to be some sensible explanation—some reason that her life was about to end today in the cold, dark Pacific Ocean. Just as blackness threatened and her vision swam, she felt something strong grasp her under her shoulders and yank her violently up and out of the water.

"Help me! Grab her legs!" Josiah Quinn pulled Zoey roughly onto his lap on his sit-on-top kayak, struggling to get her out of the water without capsizing himself. Fear gripped his heart as he worked to save her. Zoey had passed out, which made it easier to lift her, but it also meant he had only seconds to save her. He didn't think she was breathing, and her limbs were lax and lifeless.

Dear God, please help her!

He quickly said the short and silent prayer as he motioned to Rick Hall, one of the other kayakers on the trip who was only a few feet away in his own boat. Mia moved her kayak back and out of the way as Rick approached. As he pulled up alongside Josiah, Rick leaned forward and grabbed Zoey's feet and pulled her lower half up, helping to secure her onto Josiah's kayak. Her eyes were closed, and her skin was a deathly white with a tinge of blue.

She wasn't breathing.

Fear and memories from his recent tour in Afghanistan filled Josiah's brain as adrenaline shot through his veins. He had lost too many soldiers under his command, especially during his last tour. He wasn't going to lose Zoey. He bent over and started CPR, focusing on getting air into her lungs. The first few breaths didn't seem to help at all, and he readjusted, tilting her head a little farther back. After the fifth attempt, she sputtered and choked as liquid came streaming out of her mouth and nose. He rolled her head to the side the best he could to help the fluid get out, then leaned closer again so he could tell if she had started breathing on her own or not. Hot moist air touched his cheek and he leaned back in relief. *Thank You, Lord!*

She was alive. She was going to make it.

More water poured out of her mouth, and once again, he tilted her to the side so it could clear her body. She was still choking and gasping for air, and he gently moved her light brown hair away from her face and held her tightly so she didn't end up back in the bay. He was so thankful she was wearing a dry suit that provided thermal insulation and kept the cold away from the majority of her skin. Otherwise, the hypothermia would have probably stolen her life.

It was a good thing he hadn't been leading this trip, Josiah thought silently as he supported her. He was only a novice in the outdoors, and although he'd led soldiers into battle, he'd never tried his skills against the harsh Alaskan wilderness. Zoey had been leading these expeditions for the last eight years and probably knew the best equipment and clothing to use, and he was instantly thankful for that expertise. That knowledge had saved her life today. Even so, a near-drowning experience could have lasting effects, and she would need to be watched very carefully for the next few hours to make sure she would be okay.

He looked quickly over to shore. Their campground was still about one hundred yards away. He needed to get her there as quickly as possible so he could help her even more.

He reached behind him and pulled a length of rope from his pack, then caught Rick's eye and threw it over to him. "Catch this. Good. Are the rest of the campers safe?"

Rick nodded, the rope in his hand. "Everyone got pretty wet, but Mia was the only one that didn't manage to stay in her boat. They're heading back to shore now to warm up and get ready for dinner."

Josiah took in this information and made a quick decision. "Good. Please tie Zoey's kayak to yours and go on back to the camp. Then get everyone to change and build a campfire, okay?" He glanced at Zoey, who seemed almost lifeless. "I need you to lead the group while I get her back and evaluate the extent of her injuries." He had reviewed all of the campers' applications and hadn't noted that anyone besides himself was trained in CPR or first aid. It was a good thing the army had taught him the basics. He needed that knowledge now as he tried to help Zoey.

Rick nodded, his expression concerned. "Will do." He floated over to Zoey's kayak, where he bent over and tied the rope to the front of her boat, then to the rear of his. Josiah also saw him retrieve Zoey's red-and-black paddle that was floating nearby. He was glad Rick had taken the time to head over and help. Mia had quickly disappeared after Josiah had arrived on the scene. The rest of the group were all heading back toward the camp at Rick's direction, sending concerned looks over their shoulders as Josiah tried to help Zoey.

Josiah grabbed his own paddle from where it had been strapped on the side of his kayak, and turned his boat toward shore, moving quickly with sure, strong strokes. He glanced at Zoey every now and then, secured in front of him, making sure the best he could that she was still alive and breathing. She coughed now and again, but he could see the faint rise and fall of her chest as the oxygen slowly returned into her system, and the bluish skin color was slowly dissipating from her face. Still, it was obvious from her coughing that her lungs hadn't cleared completely yet, and he wanted to get her safely back to camp as soon as possible.

Was Mia to blame for Zoey's current condition? It was hard for him to tell exactly what had been happening when he arrived on the scene. Mia was a diminutive woman with hawklike dark eyes and bleach-blond hair. She wore perfect makeup, had long, decorated fingernails and seemed out of place in this wilderness setting. She sure didn't seem tough enough to hurt anyone, but he knew size could be deceptive. Even smaller people could be fit and incredibly strong, and by all appearances, Mia spent quite a bit of time in the gym. Had Mia been trying to drown Zoey? When he had first arrived on the scene, it had looked as if she was pushing Zoey beneath the water. But why would she want to do such a thing? It was unthinkable. And yet...

Zoey moaned and moved slightly, and Josiah doubled his efforts to swiftly get her back to shore. He could see the rest of the group up ahead of him already reaching the campground and he did a quick count of the people who were kayaking as part of the expedition team. All

nine guests were accounted for, and he saw Rick directing them as they pulled their boats ashore and moved
among the cabins.

As Josiah covered the last bit of distance, he reflected
on what had brought him to this point. The group had
just set out today on a fourteen-day kayak expedition.
All nine of the campers worked at the Western Office
Supply and Tech Solutions store in Seacrest, California, and were here on a company retreat that had been
planned almost a year in advance. Zoey usually led
the trips by herself, but Josiah had joined them at the
last minute after his final army discharge paperwork
had come through. He was now officially retired at the
rank of major. He'd planned to make a career of the
army, but now he was facing an entirely different future. Unfortunately, while serving in Afghanistan, he
had sustained an injury to his left leg during a mortar
attack, and the army had quickly retired him since he
could no longer pass his physical fitness test. At first,
the doctors thought he wouldn't walk again, but Josiah
had surpassed all expectations and had slowly recovered enough to walk with a cane. Three weeks ago, he
had left the cane behind as well.

Despite his physical improvement, the injury had
been a huge blow to his career plans, and he found
himself floundering at times. He'd loved the military.
To him, it was more than a job—it was a way of life.
Now, faced with an entirely different and unplanned future, he struggled to find a path forward. This trip had
been a great excuse to come to Alaska for a change in
scenery and a chance to regroup. He'd also put God on

the back burner over the last several years, which had been a mistake. He hoped to reconnect to his faith during the days ahead.

Tikaani Tours Inc. had belonged to his father, Chase Quinn, but ownership had passed to him upon his father's death a couple of months ago, along with several other companies. Josiah had never thought he'd actually hold the reins to any of these businesses, but with his father's death and his own injury, his life had taken an unexpected turn, and now it was time to start learning the ropes. He'd decided to start with Tikaani, which was the smallest of his father's operations, and then gradually learn how to manage and maintain the success of all of the other companies. While his father had been alive, Josiah had spent little time with Tikaani or any of the other businesses, and he realized he had a lot to learn. When he'd first arrived in Alaska a short time ago, he'd thought his physical fitness training and army survival skills would be enough to prepare him for this trip, but now he wasn't so sure. Danger lurked around every corner and surviving his army tour was vastly different from the skills he needed in the Alaskan wilderness.

Now that he was the owner and operator of the company, it behooved him to learn how everything worked and connect with the staff. He was meticulous with details and driven to succeed, just like his father had been, but he didn't have a background in business, so he knew he had his work cut out for him. Chase Quinn had been an amazing entrepreneur who had amassed a small fortune during his lifetime. Even though his father had sold off his shares of some of his companies about six months before his death, he had still owned a large portfolio. Josiah actually wasn't that familiar with many of his father's holdings, but he realized it was time that he stepped up to the plate and started managing his new assets. In Afghanistan, he'd always been a hands-on boss with every mission. Running Tikaani Tours would be no exception. He had quite a job to do—living up to the level of excellence his father had achieved—and like it or not, handling the great man's legacy had now become his new vocation. It was a daunting task, and one he still wasn't sure he could manage. His father had been a demanding and task-oriented parent. Chase Quinn had never accepted failure and had constantly pushed his son to succeed. Even now, after his father's death, he felt enormous pressure to successfully continue his father's legacy.

He thought back over the last few hours. A larger boat had delivered them all to the first campsite, and after setting up and going through a safety lesson, the group had eagerly gone for a kayak trip to the nearby glacier. It had been a momentous occasion, and one none of them would likely ever forget. Besides the stark beauty of the glacier, they'd even seen a humpback whale on their trip across the bay, and it had been truly exciting to see the huge animal only a few yards away and hear it exhale from its blowhole. The whale even appeared to be putting on a show for the tourists. It swam playfully by the kayaks, diving, resurfacing, then plowing its open mouth across the surface through a bed of kelp to feed.

Watching it made Josiah feel profoundly small and insignificant. Alaska was vastly different from Afghanistan. Everything here was quiet, colorful, large and strangely peaceful. He was used to sand, noise and busyness. Yet even so, he loved the rugged beauty of the place and was considering making Alaska his permanent home.

But could he do it? Could he make a life for himself outside of the military in this stark wilderness? Would managing his father's remaining businesses be enough to make him happy? Would he be able to live up to his father's expectations? Doubt surfaced as the various thoughts ran through his mind. His father had not been an easy man to please, and Josiah had struggled his entire life to make the older man proud. Now his father was dead. Would Josiah be able to maintain the man's legacy?

Zoey sputtered again and moved restlessly, and his thoughts instantly returned to the care and safety of his passenger. Suddenly she jerked and his kayak tilted dangerously to the right, almost swamping it. Water poured over the side and splashed over both of them, then rolled to the bottom of the kayak and out the scupper holes. Josiah grabbed her with one arm the best he could, trying to secure her and hold on to his paddle at the same time. She lurched again and he looked around anxiously to yell for help from someone, but all of the other campers were still too far away and there was no one nearby to assist him. His heartbeat surged against his chest as fear for her well-being swept over him. He quickly compensated and moved to the left to keep the boat from swamping, then wrapped his left leg over her legs, anchoring her to both him and the boat. Was he going to lose her?

Josiah said a silent prayer, hoping God was listening. Then he bent close to her ear. "Zoey, you're gonna be okay. Hold still. Try to stay in the kayak." He softened his voice as much as he could, hoping it would soothe her as he adjusted her. He wanted to keep her as comfortable as possible while also keeping her safe. He wasn't even sure she was cognizant enough to understand him, but he kept murmuring in her hear. "That's it. You're going to be okay. Just rest."

She coughed and sputtered but seemed to calm somewhat as he continued to speak softly. Finally, she quit pulling against him and relaxed. He realized a near-drowning experience could make someone disoriented and agitated, and that was obviously what was happening here. He had met Zoey a few times over the years, but he didn't know her that well. Still, he had always been impressed by her professionalism and dedication to detail. If she was in full control of her faculties, she would probably be teaching him the best way to get an injured person back to camp instead of struggling against his hold.

Zoey moaned. "My chest hurts." She opened her eyes, but Josiah wasn't sure she was really registering him or whether or not she even realized what was happening or why.

"Yes, that's normal," Josiah soothed. "Just hold still. We're almost back at the camp."

"My kayak…" She motioned with her hand. "I can't leave it out there in the bay."

Her voice was raspy, and she coughed again. There was still a gurgling sound coming from her throat, testifying to the excess water that was still in her body.

"Don't worry. We've taken care of it. Rick already towed it to shore." He continued to paddle—only fifty yards now until they would reach the rocky beach. He kept talking, hoping that his voice was helping the situation. She certainly seemed calmer. He kept on. "He got your paddle, too, and all of the other campers are safe." He paused. "You'll probably hurt for a few days, but then you'll start feeling a lot better. Even though we got you out of that icy water, I still want to get you back to camp as soon as we can. You need to get warmed up. Your skin is still a little blue, and I want to make sure your core temperature gets back to normal and you're getting enough oxygen."

He wasn't sure any of this information was actually getting through to her, but he kept talking the rest of the way back to the campground, just as he had encouraged other wounded soldiers during the attack that had ultimately injured his leg. What he didn't want was her wrenching out of his grip again and ending up back in the water.

A few minutes later, he safely navigated back to shore and was met by Rick and several other campers. They helped him carry Zoey to her cabin while others secured and stored his kayak. Rick had already taken care of Zoey's kayak when he first returned. There were ten cabins in all circling a clearing where a large campfire was already burning in the middle. Flames licked at the sky that was just turning to dusk in a cascade of pale blues and pinks. If Zoey hadn't been hurt, it would have been the perfect ending to a perfect day. Mia followed the group as they carried Zoey, her eyes concerned, her voice sharp. "Is she going to be okay? Has she said anything? Does she remember what happened?"

She didn't get an immediate response and tugged anxiously on Josiah's sleeve.

"Hey, I asked you a question. Is she going to make it?"

Josiah glanced in her direction as he adjusted his hands on Zoey's shoulders. "I'm sure she will be fine, but she won't be up to holding a conversation for a while." He still wasn't sure what to think of the woman. Was she a friend or foe? What had actually happened out there?

"I think she hit her head on the kayak when she was trying to flip mine over," Mia said quickly. "I sure hope she's going to recover. I can't believe she almost drowned!" She paused. "It sure was a good thing you were close enough to help out."

Was that a touch of sarcasm in her voice? Josiah wasn't sure. He glanced in her direction a second time as they continued to Zoey's cabin. She had a sincere look of regret on her face, but her tone contradicted her expression.

Or was he being too sensitive?

After all, he didn't know these people, and perhaps Mia always acted like this. Zoey's experience looked like an accident, but now Josiah was beginning to wonder. Still, what possible motive could Mia have to hurt Zoey?

TWO

Zoey groaned as pain radiated throughout her head and limbs. She remembered trying to help Mia with her kayak, but not much else that happened afterward. She raised her hand and gingerly felt the large bump on the right side of her head. Had she been hit by the boat in her attempt to get Mia to safety? How did she end up in her cabin?

"Welcome back," Josiah said softly.

Zoey looked over at the man who was sitting next to her, reading a paperback novel. A small lamp was sitting on the table by his chair, and he had changed and was wearing jeans and a thick red flannel shirt instead of his dry suit. His short, brown, military-styled hair was spiky as if he'd run his fingers through it a time or two, and his dark brown eyes studied her intently. A wave of surprise and confusion swept over her. What was he doing in her cabin? "I've got a really bad headache. Did something happen? What are you doing here?"

"That headache is no surprise. I'm not sure how you got hurt, but you ended up in the water and nearly drowned."

Zoey frowned. "I don't remember much. Did you bring me here?" Her sentence ended with a bout of coughing, and he quickly set aside his book, then hurriedly leaned over and helped her sit up. The new angle helped, and once she caught her breath, he eased her back down. He had covered her with blankets and removed her dry suit, but she could tell she was still wearing her bathing suit that she always wore underneath.

"I did. Like I said, you nearly drowned. Rick helped me get you out of the water, I did CPR and I've been watching over you for a couple of hours now." He reached over and touched her forehead. "Your temperature seems back to normal, and your color is a lot better. You were kind of blue when we first got you here." He leaned back. "I tried to use the radio to call a doctor and make sure I was doing everything necessary to help you, but all I got was static. When you're feeling better, maybe you can train me again on how to contact the home base."

"Yeah, I'll do that," she said softly. Embarrassment swept over her from head to toe and she felt her cheeks heating. She was a professional tour guide. How had she gotten into such a deadly predicament? Josiah was the new owner of the company. He had to know about the complaint that had been lodged against her during her last trip. It had been a bogus criticism, and the camper had been difficult to deal with throughout his expedition. Even so, his vicious written attack had surprised her and had even made the local news in the nearby small town of Lynx Creek. The coverage couldn't have been good for business. She'd never had such a horrible experience with someone. In fact, most of her campers left her excellent reviews on all of the social media platforms. There had been no pleasing that man, however, no matter what she did. He'd started out with complaints about the food and equipment they were using and had a negative comment to share nearly every time she approached him. By the end of the trip, he was even complaining about the lack of wildlife they'd seen and the speed of the river water. His problems bordered on the ridiculous, but she had still tried everything within her power to please him. Zoey has been working at Tikaani for over eight years, and her reputation and professionalism were so good that she'd been operating with total control of the expeditions and very little input from the home office or Josiah's father. Now Josiah was here in the flesh and probably deciding during this trip not only how closely he needed to supervise her but also whether or not she should even keep her job.

Frustration filled her. She had met Josiah a couple of times over the years, but he was still virtually a stranger. Yet now this man whom she barely knew held her future in the palm of his hand. He'd never even been on a tour before! She remembered he'd spent time in the army, but it had always been his father, Chase Quinn, whom she had worked hard to impress. Her efforts had paid off, and she had earned the right to manage these expeditions. Leading these tours was usually considered man's work by most people in the industry, but she had surpassed all expectations and proved herself and her abilities. Now everything she had worked so hard for was slowly slipping through her fingers, and apparently, Josiah alone would now decide her future.

Having to prove herself anew was a bitter pill to swallow.

She glanced at his brown eyes, trying to interpret his expression. Was there recrimination there? Frustration? Pity? Was he upset about the recent complaint and holding it against her? There wasn't enough light to tell, or maybe he was just difficult to read. Or maybe she was just so worn-out after her ordeal that she wasn't able to get an accurate notion about what he was thinking. Regardless, being flat on her back when she was supposed to be leading the excursion couldn't be a good thing.

"I'm sorry you had to step in. I wish I could tell you exactly what happened…"

He shook his head. "Shhh. It's okay. We can talk about it later if you want, but right now, I just want you to rest. Are you hungry?"

She blinked. That didn't sound like something you would say to someone if you were planning to fire them. Still, she needed to be extra careful during this trip and make sure that she was at the top of her game. Nearly drowning on the first day couldn't have made a favorable impression.

He held out a plate to her that had been sitting on the table by the lamp. "It's not much—just a bran muffin and some dried fruit. I wasn't sure how much your stomach could handle, if anything. You swallowed a lot of seawater."

Her belly rumbled at the sight. She wasn't sure of the time, but her body was telling her that dinner had come and gone, and she needed some nourishment. She sat up again and took the plate. "Thanks. I didn't realize how hungry I was until you showed me the food."

He turned slightly and handed her a travel mug that had also been resting on the table. "I wasn't sure if coffee or tea was your thing either, so I opted for hot apple cider."

She shrugged. "The cider is fine. I'm not fussy, and actually, I'm the one who makes up the menus, so I like pretty much all the food and drinks that we take on these trips." She swallowed hard, then took a sip of the cider. "It feels like I shouldn't be thirsty since I still feel kind of bloated, but my throat is sore and my mouth seems like it's full of cotton."

"That's normal." He took the mug from her and set it back on the table as she tore off a piece of the muffin and ate slowly. He leaned back in his chair. "What do you know about these campers?"

She drew her lips into a thin line. "Nothing more than the normal information they send in when they book a trip. I read through their registration materials so I could make work assignments, but nothing out of the ordinary stood out. They all work at the same store in California in different capacities, a place called Western Office Supplies and Tech Solutions, and they're here on a work retreat. They signed up about a year ago but canceled their first reservation and then rescheduled. They each come from different divisions within the company."

He nodded, taking in the information. "I've heard of Western. My father was actually a shareholder for a while, and I think he used to give a big discount to companies that he owned an interest in if they would send their employees on a Tikaani Tour."

"He still gave them the discount," Zoey confirmed. "But I think he told me he sold those shares a while ago."

Josiah nodded. "That's correct. He sold them a few months before he died."

Zoey coughed. "Well, Tikaani gets most of its business through either your father's old connections or the various social media platforms. He spent a lot of time building and maintaining relationships with people." She took another bite as she studied Josiah. He was clearly worried about something, and she wondered if they were about to discuss that awful camper and his complaint. She stiffened, preparing to defend herself and her actions, if needed. "What's on your mind?"

He exhaled, then looked her in the eye. "I don't know for sure, but I think Mia Phillips might have been trying to kill you."

"What? Kill me?" Her blue eyes rounded and he could tell he'd shocked her, but he was a straightforward guy and there was no reason to beat around the bush. "Why would she do such a thing? I don't even know her. I'd never even seen her before this morning."

"I have no idea why, but the whole episode out in the bay doesn't make sense. She claimed you hit your head on the boat, but from a distance, it looked like she hit you pretty hard with her own paddle. And when I came to help, it seemed like she was trying to drown you. I could have sworn she was trying to hold you under the water."

"That's ludicrous!"

He shrugged. He agreed the idea seemed absurd, but he had seen what he had seen. "I know it sounds that way, but her behavior seemed extremely aggressive, and there's more. After I got you back to shore, she was really concerned about whether or not you remembered anything. It was as if she was scared that you might reveal what actually happened out there."

"Maybe she was just concerned?"

He rubbed his forehead and grimaced. "Sure, I guess that could be it, but that's not what my instincts tell me, and my gut is usually right. The whole incident and her behavior just seem pretty strange." He pursed his lips. "Do you have any enemies?"

It was Zoey's turn to shrug. "None that I know of. I've been running these tours for the last eight years, and beyond that, I don't socialize much. I work with the campers, but we're only together for two weeks, and then a new tour arrives. It's not enough time to develop friendships or enemies." She rubbed her left temple. "I do know I've never seen Mia before this morning. She's a total stranger."

"Well, I think we should keep an eye on her for the rest of this trip, just in case. It won't hurt to be on your guard around her." He looked at Zoey carefully, trying to assess her current condition, despite the poor lighting. She was eating and drinking and seemed to be in complete control of her faculties. Her cheeks were a rosy pink again, and her voice, while hoarse, had lost that gurgling quality. He was no doctor, but his first-aid training made him confident that she was going to be okay and no worse for wear. "That is…" He raised an eyebrow.

"That is what?" Her tone became a bit defensive, and it surprised him. He pushed forward anyway.

"That is unless we need to call the base camp and have you taken back there to recuperate?"

"No, thank you. I'm fine, Mr. Quinn. I appreciate your help, but I'm perfectly able to continue as the leader of this trip."

He frowned, surprised at the steel in her tone. What was going on here? Had he offended her? That certainly hadn't been his intention. His only thought was for her welfare. "What happened to Josiah?"

She straightened and met his eyes. "Josiah, I am perfectly able to continue. You don't need to nurse me any longer. Thank you for your help, but I can handle my responsibilities." She looked away and smoothed the blankets with her hand, back and forth, erasing the creases. She was obviously nervous or scared, and he wasn't sure why. All he was doing was verifying she was well enough to continue. Still, she had been through enough today, and he didn't want to broach a subject that was clearly making her more uncomfortable.

He put up his hands. "Okay. Just checking. I'll leave you to rest and will see you tomorrow morning." He moved to leave but then paused. "Promise me you'll watch out for Mia? I may be totally out in left field here, but she worries me."

Zoey nodded. "I promise," she agreed. "I'd rather be safe than sorry."

He left her cabin and made his way to his own, playing the last bits of their conversation back in his mind. *Had* he offended her somehow? He sure didn't want to upset her. Zoey basically ran Tikaani Tours. He needed her help if he was going to keep the business up and running. His thoughts were immediately scattered when he heard angry voices up ahead. He turned away from the campfire and his cabin and moved toward the voices, using his flashlight to illuminate the path into the woods. He couldn't make out their words, but two men were clearly arguing and unhappy. As he got closer, their voices got louder and more agitated. When he came upon the scene, Marty Garcia and John Webster, two of the campers, who both appeared to be in their fifties or so, were standing inches apart, their hands fisted. Both had red faces with angry expressions. Josiah wondered fleetingly if they would have hurt each other if he hadn't arrived at that exact moment. They looked as if they were about to have a fistfight.

"You two okay?" Josiah asked, holding his flashlight above his head and pointed directly at his quarry, just as the military had taught him.

Marty was the first to back down. He took a step back and crossed his arms. "Yeah, we're fine. Just a difference of opinion."

Josiah turned to John. "That true, John?"

John Webster took a bit longer to get himself under control, but he finally managed it. "I guess. It's time for bed anyway. Maybe tomorrow, things will go a bit smoother." He pushed by Josiah and headed back toward the cabins. A few moments later, Marty followed him.

"See you tomorrow, Quinn."

"Yeah," Josiah replied, watching them go. Had everyone totally lost it in the last two hours? He made his way back to his cabin, limping heavily. His war injury seemed to hurt him at the most inconvenient times, and this was definitely one of them. He rubbed the thigh muscle that was tight and throbbing under his jeans and grimaced. Shrapnel from an injury he received in Afghanistan had caused nerve damage to his leg, and he seemed to alternate between pain and times when the limb refused to function. It was extremely frustrating, but he knew, in the grand scheme of things, he had little to complain about. Many had lost their lives. He could still see, hear, walk and talk. Despite the discomfort, he considered himself blessed in spite of his injury. He still continued to do physical therapy and exercises to work his leg, but that was a small price to pay for regaining his ability to walk.

What he didn't like was starting over. He'd planned to make a career of the army. Now he was forced to consider different possibilities and make a new plan for his life. He had options, but he wasn't a spontaneous guy and he didn't like change, especially when it was thrust upon him.

He made it back to his cabin but had trouble getting to sleep. Usually, if sleep wouldn't come, it was because he was wrestling with visions and memories of losing soldiers in his command. But this time, it wasn't Afghanistan that occupied his thoughts. Instead, visions of Zoey with a smile on her face filled his mind. She was laughing in the cool Alaskan sun and pointing at humpback whales, delight shining in her eyes.

He thought back to his last relationship. He had dated Mindy Carter for over a year and had been considering asking her to marry him when he'd discovered she was cheating on him. Mindy was beautiful but apparently also had a heart as cold as ice. When he had confronted her, she hadn't even asked for forgiveness or explained her actions. She'd just gotten up and left him sitting at their favorite restaurant, his heart shattered into little pieces. She took with her all of the plans he had made. A home together, starting a family, everything… Now he was truly starting from scratch—both in his personal life and in his professional one.

Josiah Quinn would never trust another woman with his heart as long as he lived.

Of that, he was certain.

THREE

Screaming tore through the air.

Zoey awoke with a start, pulled on her pants and shoes, grabbed her coat and tumbled out of her cabin. The shrieking didn't stop. If anything, it got louder and sent a cold chill down her spine. She broke into a run and headed toward the sound, and was instantly joined by Josiah and Lucas Phillips, Mia's husband, who had also just come out of their cabins. While Josiah looked cool and unflustered, Lucas seemed disheveled.

"What's going on?" Lucas demanded as he tried to button his flannel shirt. "What's all the screaming about?"

"I have no idea," Zoey answered as they headed toward the other side of the camp where Patricia was standing near another cabin, still screaming. It was almost seven in the morning, and the air was crisp and cool. Pale pink and yellow light bounced off the nearby water and reflected the sun that was just beginning to top the trees.

Zoey arrived first and took Patricia's arms and tried to steady her. The woman was shaking and barely in control, but she didn't seem to be in any danger. Zoey checked her over for blood or a wound of some sort but saw no visible injuries. From the sound of the woman's distress, Zoey had expected to see something severe. "Are you okay? What's happening? Why are you screaming?"

Patricia took several deep breaths and tried to calm herself, but it was a futile effort. Her skin was pale and her entire body was trembling. Finally, she just pointed at the cabin beside her. "He's dead!" she exclaimed with a wail.

After everything that had happened yesterday and being jolted out of bed this morning, Zoey had to struggle to remember whose cabin Patricia was pointing at. Who had died? She glanced over at Josiah, who met her gaze. Wordlessly, Zoey released Patricia, and she and Josiah moved to the front of the cabin and he pulled open the door. Zoey could see a body lying on the sleeping bag but still couldn't identify the camper. Several of the others suddenly arrived on the scene, all in various stages of readying for their day. Most were dressed, but a few looked rather tousled and sleepy as they had run straight from their cabins to see what all the screaming was about. They crowded around the cabin, trying to peer in around the door behind her.

None were prepared for what awaited them. Josiah caught John Webster's eye. "Get everyone to step back, please."

As John shrugged and complied, Josiah and Zoey stepped inside the cabin.

Marty Garcia was lying on his back, his feet near

the cabin door, his head at the top of his sleeping bag. He was still dressed as he had been the day before, but now there was something very different about his appearance.

A large, wicked-looking Bowie hunting knife protruded from his chest, and blood had pooled in a large circle around the wound and spread out along the floor of the cabin, seeping into the sleeping bag as well as the backpack and pillow that were near the body. His skin was a pasty white, and his face still wore an expression of surprise.

Zoey's heart clenched. Poor Mr. Garcia! She barely knew the man, but no one deserved to be stabbed to death. Her first thought was to check his pulse, and just as the idea flitted across her mind, Josiah bent forward and reached for the man's wrist. She held her breath, hoping for the best, but her hopes were dashed as he reached over and closed the man's wide, unblinking eyes. Still, she glanced at Josiah, seeking confirmation. He subtly shook his head in response.

The man was definitely dead.

She'd never had a camper die during one of her trips before, or even get seriously injured. But this was more than a death caused by natural causes or some accident out on the water.

This man had clearly been murdered.

"Someone killed him!" Patricia wailed behind them. She was still outside the cabin but peering in through the open door. "I came to get him to help make breakfast, and he didn't answer when I called, so I opened his door and found him that way. He's been stabbed! Who would do such a thing?" Her voice carried throughout the compound and the other campers murmured among themselves. Patricia took a step back and started pacing in front of the cabin, and several of the campers shrank out of her way as she started flailing her arms. "I can't believe he's been murdered! We're out in the middle of nowhere!"

Josiah and Zoey ignored Patricia and glanced around the small cabin interior, but there was really nothing else to see. Mr. Garcia had been killed before he'd even had a chance to unpack his backpack. Zoey wasn't an expert investigator, but she didn't see any clues that suggested who the culprit might be. No footprints marred the floor, and the rest of the cabin was empty except for the table and two chairs on the other side of the room. Even the Bowie knife itself wasn't helpful. Most of the campers carried a knife of some sort, and the murder weapon could have belonged to anyone. They could still bag the blade for the authorities, though. Maybe the knife had fingerprints on it, or some other piece of telltale evidence that wasn't readily apparent. They exited the cabin and Josiah closed the door firmly behind him, then they turned and faced the group.

"Marty Garcia is dead. Everyone needs to step away from this cabin until we can call this in to the base camp and get further instructions," Zoey declared. She glanced over at Josiah, whose expression was grim. He had his hands on his hips and his lips were drawn into a tight line. "We need to get help from law enforcement. Josiah, do you want to join me while I make the call?"

He nodded in response, then noticed Rick in the

group and met his eye. "Rick, stay here and guard the door while we're gone. I want to make sure nobody tampers with the crime scene."

Rick did as he was asked, and Josiah and Zoey headed toward Zoey's cabin as the group slowly dispersed behind them. Zoey glanced from face to face as she passed, examining their expressions. Most showed shock or horror, but a few seemed to show anger, and Mia showed no emotion at all. John Webster even had a bland countenance that seemed devoid of any reaction. If anything, he seemed annoyed, as if he had been awoken from a wonderful dream and was now ready to curl up again and go back to sleep. Was the man's death simply an inconvenience to him? She thought back to Josiah's words of warning from yesterday. Had Mia killed Marty Garcia? If not her, then who? And what possible motive could someone have? She glanced back to look at Webster again, but he had already returned to his own cabin. Maybe Mia wasn't the only one on this trip they should be worrying about. Trepidation swept over her.

The communication equipment was stored in Zoey's cabin, and once inside, she quickly turned on the radio and pulled out the mic. "Base one, this is Trip one, come in."

Nobody answered. Usually, someone responded immediately. She tried a couple more times but was met with only static. She turned and looked at Josiah, who was standing silently behind her. There was no cell service out here due to the remoteness of the location, and the high frequency radio was the only method of communication they had with the base camp beyond a backup handheld radio that allowed short texts. They were in the wilderness of the backcountry in Alaska, and even the boat that had dropped them off yesterday wouldn't be returning until the next expedition.

"Has this ever happened before?" Josiah asked.

"I've never had a camper killed, if that's what you're asking," Zoey replied as she tried once again to get through.

"No," Josiah replied. "What I meant is, have you ever had trouble contacting the base camp?"

"It's rare, but it happens," Zoey responded. "Sometimes there are storms near the home base that knock out the satellite towers, and we lose communication for a day or two. Usually, I just continue on our trip and keep the news to myself, and everything turns out okay. I don't want to worry the campers unnecessarily. Eventually contact is restored and no one is the wiser."

"Do you think this static is being caused by a storm as well?"

"That's my best guess," Zoey replied. "And if some bad weather hit the base camp, the storm may be coming this way. Weather up here can change pretty quickly. I think it behooves us to start moving, rather than waiting, even though Mr. Garcia is dead. If we don't, we could get stuck up here."

"Is there any way to contact law enforcement directly? We need crime scene investigators up here as soon as possible."

Zoey shook her head. "No, we're too remote. We are literally out in the middle of nowhere. The base camp would normally contact the police for us, if we could get a hold of them, but even the best plans fail when Mother Nature steps in." She shifted. "Even though we can't get a detailed message through, we do have a special communication set up with the base camp so we can notify them in case of emergencies. I can send an SOS message with my handheld high frequency radio. I just can't give many details—I'm restricted to 160 characters. At least that message will give the base camp a heads-up that we've got a problem, though. They know to alert the authorities when they get a message like that. We'll keep the handheld radio with us as we travel and can give the base camp short updates until full communication is restored. At least that way, they'll be aware of what we're dealing with as well as our GPS coordinates. Once we get farther down the mountain, we can hopefully get a better connection and can contact them with more details. Then law enforcement can send up some help."

Josiah put his hands on his hips. "What about contacting the boat captain that dropped us off yesterday? Can't he just come back and pick us up? We haven't even started down the river yet."

"No, he's long gone and way too far away by now. He won't be returning to this neck of the woods until the next tour begins, and that's a month away. We could stay here and wait for him, but it would be faster to head down the river following our normal course. And if the weather does get bad up here, too, we'll be sorry we stayed." She sighed. "Even if a storm isn't heading for us, I still think our best bet is to keep moving toward the rendezvous point. Trying to get back to civilization as soon as possible seems like the best option." She looked up at Josiah, wondering what he was thinking. She could offer advice, but ultimately, he was the new owner of Tikaani Tours, and the decision was his. "What do you want to do?"

Josiah paced back and forth for a bit, then turned and faced Zoey again. His face was firm, and she could see his military bearing in his stance and features. "I agree with you," he said softly. "And I think we need to keep our communication issues quiet. We don't need that group out there panicking, and that's exactly what they'll do if they think we're cut off from the rest of the world without any help on the way."

"I think it's too late to keep them from panicking," Zoey said, shaking her head. "Patricia is already totally out of control, and her fear is contagious. But even if we can keep them calm, what do we do with Mr. Garcia? His cabin and this whole campground are a crime scene."

Zoey wrapped her arms around her middle, trying to keep her hands from shaking. She couldn't remember the last time she'd been scared during one of these trips, but now, for the first time, anxiety poured through her veins. They were out in a remote part of Alaska with no communication with the outside world, and no help from law enforcement.

And one of her campers was a murderer.

Josiah suddenly felt the urge to comfort Zoey and wipe the look of distress off her face, but when he took a step forward, she immediately took a step away and shrank back, almost as if she was afraid of him. Did she think he was going to hurt her?

Did she think he was the killer?

The idea seemed preposterous, but there had to be some reason she didn't want him too close to her. He was also surprised at his own feelings. Where had that impulse to comfort her come from? After Mindy, he had promised himself he would never get close to a woman again, yet here he was, trying to console someone who obviously didn't want comforting. He filed those thoughts away to ponder later and tried to stay focused on the immediate problem. He had commanded troops in Afghanistan but had never been involved in criminal investigations before. The army had a totally separate unit that performed that function.

He paced some more as thoughts swirled in his mind. They were in a remote location. There was no help available. And someone had just murdered one of their campers. He wondered fleetingly what his father would have done if he hadn't died five months ago. The man had been a brilliant businessman and had always had a take-charge attitude, no matter what issue or problem arose. Josiah had always tried to emulate his father. The ability to command hadn't come easily to him, but his dad had constantly pushed him to succeed, and ultimately, it was that drive that had been instilled in him since an early age that had made him a successful military commander. He had loved his father, even though their relationship had been rocky at times. Honoring Chase Quinn through continuing that legacy was his new immediate goal. So, what would his father have done in this situation?

Unfortunately, today, his father wasn't here to ask.

He wished he'd had the chance to spend more time with the man. Unfortunately, by the time he was an adult, he and his dad had both been so busy that they really only saw each other on the odd holiday. He regretted that fact, and now it was too late to fix it. He glanced back at Zoey, who was waiting patiently for his decision. He needed to stop woolgathering and focus on the problem at hand.

"Send out the SOS," Josiah directed as he made his decision. "That's better than nothing. Then we should take as many pictures of the crime scene as we can to aid the investigators and store the knife in a plastic bag. After that, let's bury Mr. Garcia. I know that's probably going to hinder the investigation, but I don't want any wild animals showing up. Then we'll do a search through everyone's belongings. Maybe we'll find some sort of clue that will lead us to the murderer." He put his hands on his hips. "The police can come back later and do a proper investigation, if it's still possible."

Zoey raised an eyebrow. "And if we don't find anything during our search?"

Josiah shrugged. "We'll head down the river as originally planned—" he narrowed his eyes "—but we'll be watching our backs the entire time."

FOUR

"I'm telling you, I heard Webster and Garcia arguing last night, and it was no little thing. They probably would have ended up in a big fight and seriously hurting each other if Josiah hadn't come along." Patricia paddled a little more to straighten the bow of her boat, then let the river move her kayak along. Her voice was loud and carried well across the water.

Jessie Chapman, one of the other female campers, nodded to Patricia as Zoey approached unnoticed behind them. Her attention was riveted on the woman who kept talking in a loud, obtrusive voice, doing nothing to conceal the conversation. "I've always wondered about Webster. He and Marty always seem to be arguing back at the store, and they both did their share of lying and cheating while running the purchasing department. In fact, Garcia was embezzling funds. I'm sure of it, and Webster was probably in on it with him. That's why the office supply store is about to go under. Total mismanagement. That's what I heard from some very reliable sources. And I've seen the embezzlement evidence myself. If he hadn't been killed, Garcia probably would have been arrested as soon as we returned to California, and maybe Webster, too."

Zoey was surprised by that piece of information and kept close enough to hear without interrupting. She wondered if Patricia really knew what she was talking about, or if she was just speculating and enjoying the fact that she had Jessie's full attention. Did she have any proof of the malfeasance she was describing? What exactly had she seen?

Zoey and Josiah had searched everyone's belongings before burying Marty Garcia's body and leaving camp this morning, but they hadn't found anything suspicious. Of course, she was no trained law enforcement officer, so she hadn't even been entirely sure what she was looking for. They had secured the knife that was used for the murder in a plastic bag and left it in the cabin where Garcia's body had been found. They'd also taken several pictures with their cell phones of the crime scene and surrounding area. There was no service this high up in the backcountry, but the cell phones could be used when they returned to the lower base camp, and they were less bulky to carry than a traditional camera, so many campers brought them along to document their adventure, even if they couldn't make calls or access the internet. The tour company also provided a community solar powered charger that made it easy for them to recharge the batteries when needed. As a result, Zoey always kept her phone handy.

Jessie gasped at Patricia's comment, and Zoey's attention returned to the campers. "Is the store going to declare bankruptcy? I'm so worried about that! Now what am I going to do? I've been working at Western for the last sixteen years. I don't even know if I can find something else at this point. I'm going to lose everything!"

"The store is going under," Patricia confirmed. "That's a fact. How long it will take—well, that's anybody's guess. I'm telling you, I know it's true. I work in the accounting department, and I see the numbers. If I were you, I'd dust off your résumé and start sending it out as soon as we get back home." She nodded effusively. "I can help you update your résumé if you want. I'm really good at that sort of thing, and I've done it for some of the others."

Jessie shook her head. "That's if we survive this trip in the first place! Who knows what will happen with a murderer along?" She leaned closer to Patricia's kayak as if sharing a confidence, but still used a loud voice when she talked. "Do you think John Webster killed Mr. Garcia?"

Patricia nodded vigorously. "It has to be him. He and Marty were fighting last night, and the next thing you know, Marty is dead. Who else would want to kill him?" She glanced around and suddenly noticed that Zoey was close enough to speak to. "Zoey, why didn't you just call in that boat that dropped us off to come back up here and get us? I don't feel safe! For all we know, Webster might murder us all in our sleep!"

Zoey paddled a little closer. "We talked about it before we set out this morning, remember? The boat is long gone and won't return until next month. The best thing to do is just keep kayaking down the river. We'll be able to meet up with our team in a couple of days, and law enforcement will do a full investigation at that time."

Patricia shifted in her kayak. "Well, you're the leader, and I know you can't control what law enforcement does or doesn't do, but I don't feel comfortable with John Webster along for the rest of this trip. I think he's the one that killed poor Mr. Garcia and he's a danger to us all. You should have made him stay at the campground so he couldn't hurt anybody else."

"Everybody is innocent until proven guilty," Zoey stated firmly. "We have no proof that John Webster is the killer, and we can't just assume that he killed Mr. Garcia without some sort of evidence that points to his guilt. We questioned everyone as thoroughly as we could, and of course no one confessed." She paddled a few strokes. "An argument the night before is not enough to make someone stay behind. This is the Alaskan wilderness. It's too dangerous for a novice to be out here alone, even if they are suspected of a crime."

"Well, you don't know the entire history," Patricia retorted. "Webster is dangerous. I'm sure of it. By allowing him to continue, you're putting all of us in danger."

Zoey grimaced. She wanted information so she could learn more about the peril they were facing, but at the same time, she didn't want to encourage Patricia to gossip and spread rumors among the group, especially if her accusations were inaccurate. What if Patricia was condemning the wrong person and her allegations were wrong? Zoey weighed the pros and cons, then pushed forward, hoping that if she asked a few more questions, it wouldn't make the problem worse. "What history are you talking about?" she asked cautiously, wanting to get a little more insight. "What makes you think he's dangerous?"

"Like I was just saying, John Webster and Marty Garcia are the reasons our store is probably closing in California. We're all going to lose our jobs, and it's all because they mismanaged the funds and stole money. He and Marty were both responsible."

"Even if they took money, that doesn't necessarily make Webster a murderer. Why would he kill Marty Garcia, especially if they were in on the embezzlement together?"

"I bet they were arguing yesterday about how to split up the money they stole. That's probably why Webster killed him. Garcia has always been a greedy person. I also think he was going to turn Webster in to law enforcement," Patricia declared. "It was just a matter of time."

"But you said they were both guilty. If that's true, then Garcia would also get in trouble if he went to the police. He wouldn't want anyone to know what he'd done," Zoey said patiently.

"Garcia thought he could rat on Webster and keep the money for himself. He thinks he covered up his own involvement in the scheme, but he's wrong."

Zoey floated a few minutes in silence, then pressed further. "Do you have any proof?" So far, she still hadn't heard anything that supported Patricia's claim that John Webster was the villain. It all seemed like a bunch of conjecture. They hadn't found any evidence so far that pointed toward Webster, or anybody else. She felt out of her depth. Yet the group was looking to her to lead them, and if there was any chance at all that they could discover who the murderer was, she wanted to try.

"There are records," Patricia said softly. "Financial records, back at the office, and I know where to find them. I saved copies of everything I found on a hard drive, and I know where to look to find more evidence, if they need it. Garcia thinks he erased everything, but he didn't. Not before I copied everything. The police are going to want to talk to me when they come to investigate. I can point them in the right direction."

"How did you come across this proof of embezzlement?" Zoey asked, intrigued.

"I work in accounting," Patricia said with a sly smile. "I see copies of everything. It all goes across my desk before it goes to the next department."

Before Zoey could ask another question, Jessie changed the subject.

"Well, I'm so nervous, I can hardly think straight," Jessie said tightly as her voice wobbled and she swallowed hard. "Webster could very well be guilty. Who is he going to kill next? It could be any one of us. We should send him back to the campground just to be safe."

Zoey took a good look at Jessie. She was probably in her mid-forties and had black wavy hair, a flawless complexion and dark brown eyes. Even though she claimed to be nervous, her body language suggested she was uncomfortable with the outdoor nature of the trip, rather than the fact that someone dangerous might be in their midst. Her hands were flawlessly manicured and her hair was perfectly coiffed. Zoey had seen many such people, both men and women, who came to Alaska and were unprepared for the rugged, physical experience of kayaking down the river. Yet Jessie was a walking contradiction. She seemed soft on the outside but appeared to have a toughness on the inside that didn't seem to mesh with her outward appearance. Could she be the murderer?

Zoey glanced over at Patricia. She was a woman in her late forties who was trying to look like she was still in her youth, and like Jessie, her designer clothes made her seem out of place in this rugged terrain. But were her traits of gossiping and needing to be the center of attention just signs of insecurity? Her mannerisms reminded Zoey of a rabbit, scurrying from one place to another without any clear direction. Could her discombobulated personality be an act that was just hiding the heart of a cold-blooded killer? Was she blaming Webster and throwing suspicion on him when she was the real culprit? Or was she innocent and just eager to get the attention she craved?

Zoey stopped herself short. Good grief! Now she was playing guessing games just like the others! She mentally shook the thoughts out of her head. What they needed was cold hard evidence—nothing less. "Law enforcement will sort it out as soon as we get back to the base camp," Zoey replied, instilling a note of confidence in her voice. "In the meantime, let's just stay focused on the trip itself and getting to our next campground." The last thing she and Josiah needed was a hysterical group of campers for the next few days. Fear made people do crazy things, and oftentimes, someone innocent ended up getting hurt as a result of a mob mentality. Zoey had her hands full just keeping everyone safe from the normal perils of doing an expedition in the Alaskan backcountry. The murder added an extra level of stress that made the trip that much more dangerous—especially for all of the novice campers who were used to living in a city away from bears, rapids and the other threats found in the great outdoors. She tried to change the subject. "The river is going to speed up a little around the next bend. Please stay close to the left side. It will be easier to navigate there."

The women both nodded and Zoey paddled away from them, wanting to make sure everyone in the group was prepared as they navigated the next stretch of river. A few minutes later, after talking to everyone, she moved her kayak to the left side herself and anchored to a tree branch, reminding each of them as they passed of the safety concerns that lay ahead.

Despite her earlier self-chastisement, she couldn't help wondering as each camper paddled by her, who was the killer? Had Mia tried to kill her yesterday in the water? And if so, had Mia also killed Mr. Garcia? Or had someone else swung the fatal blow? Was John Webster an embezzler trying to cover up his crimes? She honestly had no idea. Granted, she didn't know any of them very well, but no one stood out as a prime suspect. Twelve more days. There would be twelve more days before they reached the base camp unless they could reach them by radio and rendezvous sooner.

Would someone else get hurt in the meantime? Was the killer making plans right now as they paddled to take out his or her next victim? And what was his or her motive? A cold chill went down Zoey's spine as she considered the possibilities.

Finally, the entire group passed her, and she nodded wordlessly at Josiah, who brought up the rear. She watched him paddle by and a wave of trepidation swept over her. Being around this man was also causing her stress. She already knew that her job was on the line. Why else would Josiah be here? He had to be worried about the future of Tikaani. But was the murder a guarantee that she needed to dust off her own résumé? Not to mention the fact that she'd almost drowned only a few hours after they'd arrived at the camp. She was surely giving him a horrible impression of her skill set.

But if she got fired, where would she go? The other wilderness outfits would definitely hear about the murder once this Tikaani expedition made it back to civilization, and the big operations had probably already heard about her bad review from her prior trip as well. Surely, no one would be willing to take on such a risky new employee. Up here, reputation was everything, and a lot of business was passed on by simple word of mouth and a positive recommendation. She loved Alaska and the rugged, unspoiled wilderness, and hated the idea of leaving it behind, but she might not have much choice, especially now that someone had died on her watch.

She also wasn't eager to rejoin society. Meeting very few new people and keeping to herself had become her sanctuary, and she valued this time during the Alaskan summer when she was able to spend most of her days in the great outdoors. She wasn't ready to let that go just yet. Maybe she needed to get to know Josiah a little better so she could discover his plans.

She pulled up her anchor and caught up with Josiah, who was still at the back of the group and well out of earshot of the other campers. He glanced in her direction and nodded, and she raised her chin in acknowledgment and then surreptitiously watched him out of the corner of her eye. His time in the military had left him with a muscular physique, and she had to admit, he was a very good-looking man, at least in her eyes. He had a square jaw and intense brown eyes that were filled with astute intelligence. She hadn't seen him smile much, but when he did, he exhibited perfect white teeth that lit up his entire face. She'd noticed he limped, and she'd heard somewhere that he'd injured his leg in the army, but that did nothing to detract from his appeal in her book. She was surprised he wasn't married and wondered if he had a sweetheart somewhere. Hopefully he did and would decide that Alaska wasn't for him. Maybe, just maybe, he would take this one kayak trip, decide she could handle it and return to whatever world he'd come from without totally destroying hers.

He suddenly looked up and caught her eye, and she gave him a smile, hoping he didn't realize she'd been staring. "Everybody doing okay?" she asked.

Josiah shrugged, apparently unaware of her perusal and contemplation. "I'm a bit frustrated by the comments that have been floating around. John Webster has basically been vilified, and I've been hearing complaints about him all up and down the line. Rumor has it he caused their business to fail in California, and they're all going to lose their jobs. Apparently, he and the victim had a falling-out. I even found them arguing last night. John Webster might be the murderer, but what if he's not? The man is innocent until proven guilty."

"I agree," Zoey said. "I'm hearing the same things. We need to keep an eye on Webster in case things get even uglier. He seems to be an introvert, and I'm not sure he'd even defend himself if the group turns on him."

Josiah was silent for a minute, then continued, "Webster did tell me he was taking this trip to get away from a difficult situation at Western Office Supply, but he wasn't specific. I'm pretty sure both he and Marty Garcia work in the purchasing department." He grimaced. "Patricia's gossiping isn't helping. I've seen her talking with different members of the group, bad-mouthing him to anyone that will listen." He paddled a bit, then turned to her again. "Do you know anything about her?"

"Not much," Zoey admitted. "She told me she works at the office supply headquarters in the accounting division and claims to have proof of Garcia's and Webster's embezzlement on a hard drive somewhere in their office. Before we arrived at the bend, I asked her to remember that Webster could be innocent, but I think she's enjoying being in the limelight too much to curb her tongue."

Josiah frowned. There would always be gossips in the world, and in his experience, most of them were insecure people who needed to pass along the chatter to make themselves feel important. He usually just tried to avoid people like that, but it would be impossible to do so on this trip when they would all be together for the next twelve days.

He glanced over at Zoey, who was paddling with ease and precision. "How are you feeling today?"

Her brow wrinkled at his question, but she didn't slow. "I'm fine. My throat is a little sore, but I'll make it."

The respect Josiah had for Zoey went up a notch. She had to be tired and hurting from her near-drowning experience, but she kept going on, despite the personal cost. He thought back to the complaint that had been lodged against her during the last trip. Why had someone criticized her so vehemently? He knew it was impossible to always make everyone happy, but the grievance had been rather vicious, and he had a hard time imagining that Zoey had performed as badly as the accuser claimed. He wondered about the specifics surrounding the incident and what had actually happened between the two.

He was also still wondering about yesterday's near-drowning incident. Had Mia been trying to drown Zoey? Had Zoey been clumsy or was his guide the victim of a random accident? Now a man had been murdered. Was Zoey still in danger as well?

The thought was disturbing, to say the least. Not only did he fear for her safety, but he was also concerned for the entire group. If something happened to her, they would all be in trouble. With no contact with

the home base, Zoey was the only one who could lead
them safely back to civilization. She was the wilderness expert. She was the one who knew the trail. Sure,
he had taken military survivalist training, but he didn't
know this environment, and he'd never led a kayak trip
of novice paddlers down a river before. He was also still
dealing with his military injuries, and he knew intuitively that with his leg still paining him, striking out
on his own or even trying to lead the group would be
a big mistake. He needed Zoey at the helm, even if he
had questions, but the protectiveness he was feeling toward her surprised him.

Suddenly, shouting erupted farther down the river,
causing all other thoughts to immediately disappear. Josiah started paddling harder to catch up with the others,
Zoey matching his speed at his side. As they rounded
a river bend, Josiah could see Rick Hall and his wife,
Janey, arguing with John Webster, their boats on either side of him, and other campers had also bunched
their kayaks around the man, keeping him from moving forward.

"What's going on here?" Zoey demanded as they arrived on the scene.

Webster's paddle was in Rick's hands and Janey had
grabbed the front of the man's kayak, so Webster was
basically at their mercy. Webster was a thin, diminutive man to start with, but now, being at the brunt of
the group's anger, he had shrunk back in his seat and
looked even smaller. His skin had paled and he wore
an expression of fear that he did nothing to conceal.

"This man is a murderer! He needs to be left behind

before anyone else gets killed," Janey explained vehemently. She turned to Zoey and glared at both her and Josiah. "If you two won't do it, then we'll do it for you."

FIVE

Josiah moved to intervene, but before he could maneuver his kayak against the current, Zoey had already pushed her boat between Webster's and Janey's, causing Janey to release the front of Webster's kayak.

"In case you haven't noticed," Zoey explained, her voice like steel, "I am in charge of this trip, and *no one* gets left behind. Not now, not ever. If Mr. Webster is the guilty party, then law enforcement will make that determination and deal with him accordingly when we get back to the base camp." She glared at Janey, and then at Rick. "*You* don't get to make that decision. And neither do *you*. Got it?"

Janey scowled. "*You* can't decide that for the group either." Her voice was acerbic.

Zoey was about to answer back, but Josiah held up his hand, stopping her. "Actually, she can," he said firmly. Even though his tone was soft, he could tell that the campers had recognized the authority in his voice. "In case you haven't noticed, we are out in the middle of nowhere, and Zoey is our guide. She is the only one who knows how to get us out of here and down to the base camp safely. You'd be wise to listen to her."

"You could do it," Rick said roughly as he shook Webster's paddle over his head. "You're the owner. Leave her here with the murderer if you want, and then you can lead us down."

"Yes, that's a solution," Jessie agreed from behind Janey's kayak. "Then at least we'd be safe."

"No, that's not the answer," Josiah responded firmly. "I'm not familiar with these woods or waterways. Zoey is the expert." He narrowed his eyes. Were these people really that obtuse? They weren't at Disney World trying to find the nearest exit. They were deep in the backcountry of Alaska. "But as you said, I am the owner of this tour company, and I'm telling you now, *no one* is getting left behind. Got it?"

"But what if he tries to kill one of us?" Rick demanded. "Then what? As the owner, are you going to protect us when he tries something?"

"I'm not a killer!" Webster suddenly declared. Despite his introverted nature, he suddenly sat up straighter, bolstered, no doubt, by having Josiah right beside him and exuding authority. When he spoke, his voice didn't waver. "I would never hurt Marty. He was my friend. We've worked together for years. I'm just as upset as you are that he was killed."

"Funny way of showing it," Rick declared. "We all heard about your argument."

"We had a disagreement. I don't deny it. But I wouldn't kill him because of it," Webster professed. "I could never hurt anyone."

"Enough," Josiah broke in. He wasn't going to hash out the whole thing here again in the court of public opinion, especially when their tempers were set on high and a mob mentality was hovering in the air. He motioned to Rick. "Give him his paddle back."

Rick looked as if he was going to argue, so once again, Josiah hardened his voice. He'd been an officer in the United States army. He'd perfected the authoritative tone. "Do it. Now."

Rick frowned but finally complied and threw the paddle in Webster's direction. The smaller man caught the paddle in midair and then used it to straighten his kayak. Then he backed his boat away from the group and started off by himself, apparently trying to put as much distance as he could between himself and the group.

Zoey maneuvered her kayak so she was blocking the other campers, apparently making sure that Webster had plenty of time to move his boat well away from the crush. Although the expressions of the group showed that no one was happy with Josiah's decision, they had, for the moment at least, accepted his authority, and they slowly started to disperse. He glanced over at Zoey as the kayaks separated and continued down the river in groups of two or three. He hadn't known her long enough to read her, but her expression didn't look pleased with the way he had handled the situation. If anything, she looked miffed. He waited a few moments for the other kayaks to all head downstream and then pulled up alongside her. Her body language screamed frustration, but he wasn't sure why. Hadn't he just solved the problem and gotten the group moving again? He'd never been an expert with reading women, but for the first time in quite a while, he was intrigued and wanted to know what this particular woman was thinking.

"Did I do something wrong?" he asked as he raised an eyebrow.

Zoey ran her tongue over her teeth. It wasn't a happy gesture. Her eyes burned into his for a moment or two, but she must have made a decision, because finally she shrugged, and when she spoke, there was no anger in her voice. "Nope. You're the boss."

She started paddling away from him, but he followed her, not letting her avoid the discussion. "You say that, but I get the feeling I didn't handle that situation as well as you would have liked." He caught up to her again and really studied her. She was magnificent in her ire. Her blue eyes blazed, and her face glowed with life. He even liked the way she crinkled her brow as she looked at him as if he were a few cards short of a full deck. It suddenly hit him that she was more than passingly pretty. Her feisty personality made her absolutely radiant.

"I didn't want you to handle it at all," she said in response, unable to keep the caustic tone out of her voice. "I know you don't think I can do this job, but I have been leading these expeditions for eight years. I've been faced with difficult campers in the past, and I am quite capable of dealing with them." She moved away from him, but he didn't let her escape. When she noticed he wasn't going to let the subject drop, she stopped and let him catch up, then brought her paddle up and across her lap and let the current carry her.

With a deep breath, she turned to face him. She didn't want an argument, but she was tired of wondering what he was thinking and when he was going to let the other shoe drop. If she was going to lose her job, she needed to start preparing herself now and face the situation head-on. Before he could say a word, she spoke. "Look, I know you're here evaluating my fitness to lead these trips, but I would appreciate it if you would just let me know right now if you're going to fire me or not. If you are, I need time to make a plan and figure out my next move."

Josiah looked genuinely confused. "Fire you? You're the most experienced guide I have at Tikaani. Why would I let you go?"

Zoey let out an exasperated sigh. "I know that you know all about that horrible camper that I had during the last trip. He did everything he could to ruin my reputation as a guide, and in this business, reputation is everything." She paddled silently for a moment. She truly enjoyed her job and couldn't imagine working anywhere else. She'd already had to work hard just to prove herself in a male-dominated field to reach her current position. And here was the new owner, another man who was handed the reins to a company he knew virtually nothing about, who now had the power to take away the job that she loved. If she'd thought it would help, she would argue or fight, but deep down she knew there really wasn't anything she could do to preserve her current position. She just hoped Josiah would give her the courtesy of an answer today, right here and right now, so she could start trying to figure out her future.

As she waited for Josiah to answer, her thoughts returned to how she had gotten here in the first place. She had originally taken this job to isolate herself from the outside world because of an abusive boyfriend. When she'd first arrived, the backwoods of Alaska had seemed like a prison, but it had gradually turned into a haven, and now she found herself loving the pure adventure of leading the expeditions. Each day was different and filled with new challenges. For eight years, she had carved a life for herself out of the deep Alaskan wilderness. She couldn't imagine returning to a regular existence in a city like the one she had left behind. She was no longer worried about running into that old boyfriend. She had found herself on the river, and over the past eight years, she had discovered a sense of strength and self-worth that no man would ever take away from her again. Yet even so, Josiah Quinn could change all of that and start her back at square one with just a few simple words.

She glanced in his direction, but apparently, he was still mulling over her words. Finally, he turned to her again. "Zoey, I admit that part of the reason I came on this trip was to see if there was any validity to the man's claims, but so far, I haven't seen anything that would make me want to make a change. I've reviewed his comments thoroughly, and the comments of the other campers from that particular trip, and from several other excursions. I even found handwritten notes that my father had left behind about your skills." He tilted his head slightly as he spoke. "Almost everyone, including my father, gave you rave reviews. You're good at your job, and one bad report doesn't change that. If I've learned anything over the years, I've learned that I can't make everybody happy. That's an impossible task." He smiled. "So, what I'm trying to say is that you'll have a job here at Tikaani for as long as you want one."

A wave of relief swept over her. "I'm so glad you looked into it. The man was really set on being miserable during the entire trip. There was just no pleasing him. I figured he'd recently had some trouble in his personal life and was taking it out on everyone around him. I was hoping the great outdoors would give him a new perspective, but if anything, he got angrier as we went along." She kept moving as other thoughts filled her head. As long as they were talking, she might as well broach the other issue that was bothering her. "Look, Josiah, I realize that you come from a military background, but if I am in charge of this trip, I need to make sure the campers know it and respect my authority. I could have handled the problem back there with Rick and Janey without your intervention."

Josiah squinted his eyes in a pained expression. "Did I step on your toes?"

"A little," Zoey admitted. "Like I said, I know you're the boss, but I need them to follow my directions without constantly looking to you for answers as we continue on this trip. If they question my authority, they might not do what's needed in an emergency situation when seconds count."

"Message received," Josiah said and nodded. "I apologize, but I can't promise it won't happen again. Until recently, I was an army officer. It's going to take me a while to break out of that mold. But I will try my best to tone it down and let you lead. That's a promise."

Zoey thought about that. Here was a man who had commanded troops in life-threatening situations, just like they were in now. He also exuded authority, just by walking by. It was how he carried himself, the way he spoke. He was confident and strong, despite the limp that dogged each step. He was an impressive person, and she was starting to wonder if it might behoove her to get to know him better. After all, he was her boss now. Developing a friendship with the man who signed her paycheck couldn't hurt. "I appreciate that. Thank you." She let a moment pass, then another. This really was beautiful country they were seeing, and she never got tired of looking at the landscape. She enjoyed the view for a few moments, then decided to take the first step toward getting to know him better right here and now. She took a deep breath, then plunged in.

"Do you feel comfortable telling me about your leg injury?"

His eyes jumped to hers and she quickly put up her hands in mock surrender, hoping she hadn't offended him by asking. "Only if it's not too personal. If I've stepped over the line, you can tell me flat out to mind my own business."

He continued paddling for a while as if considering her question, but finally answered. "I was leading a supply convoy in Afghanistan when it was attacked by a faction of Al-Qaeda. They fired mortars at us and one hit the truck I was riding in. Shrapnel caught me in my thigh and caused nerve damage. They weren't sure I would walk again, but I made it my mission in life to prove the doctors wrong." He stopped paddling for a moment and rubbed his bad leg as if remembering. "Unfortunately, army officers have to be physically fit to keep their jobs, and this injury meant I couldn't stay in the army, so they gave me a medical discharge and sent me on my way."

She let that sink in for a minute. Here she was worried about her job, and he'd just lost his entire vocation due to something that was totally not his fault. She felt his loss keenly, even though she didn't know him that well. It was obvious that being in the army had been more than a job to him. "Do you miss it?"

"What, army life? Having dust coat every square inch of everything I own? Eating tasteless dehydrated food in the middle of the crazy hot desert?" When she nodded, he breathed out heavily and laughed to himself. "I sure do. I really liked the army. There's structure and a sense of order to everything we do. I was planning on making it my career." He fisted his hands. "Now I have to face a very different future." He smiled, but it was a sad expression. "I'm not good at making life-altering changes. I'd wanted to be an army officer ever since middle school. Getting retired early was devastating."

He had a killer smile, even though it was tinged with dejection. It changed the whole countenance of his face and made him look friendly and approachable. Zoey looked away. She didn't want to be noticing his smile, or any of the man's features, for that matter. "Wow.

When I was in middle school, and even high school, I didn't have a clue what I wanted to do. I'm impressed that you had it all figured out."

Josiah nodded. "Yet here you are, doing what you love, right?"

"I do love it," Zoey agreed. "I just didn't plan it. Sometimes God can lead you in a direction you don't expect."

"Well, what *did* you plan to do?"

She paddled in thought for a few minutes. As a rule, she didn't share much with others, especially not men. Her previous abusive relationship had taught her men couldn't be trusted, and now, even several years later, she was still dealing with the fallout. But again, if she was going to work with this man as her boss, she had to do something to develop a friendship, and letting him know a little personal information about her was needed. Since he had shared, a little quid pro quo was warranted.

"All I knew was that I wanted to be involved in something physical. I can't stand sitting behind a desk all day. I need to be out and doing something." She looked to the side, remembering. "I was an athlete in high school and played on the basketball and softball teams. They even started a girls' flag football team my senior year, and I played on that team as well. Then I got a basketball scholarship and went to Stanford."

"Wow," Josiah said with a whistle. "From what I hear, they have a great program. What position did you play?"

"Point guard."

He tilted his head again. "Aren't point guards the

team leaders? The ones that hold the whole thing to-gether?"

She nodded. "Yep. We had a great team and ended up in the top ten for three of the four years that I was there. It was an awesome experience."

"So how did you end up here?"

Zoey stilled. She didn't share that part of her life. Not with anyone. One of the perks of this job was only having to talk to people for a few days who she knew would soon return home and forget all about her. Con-versations stayed superficial, and that was just the way she liked it. Still, Josiah was her boss. She stuck to the basics without giving any details. "I was going to teach physical education and coach basketball at the college level, but I ended up changing my mind and leaving California," she hedged. "Once I got to Alaska, I found this job and got my master's degree at the local univer-sity during the off season."

"What about a doctorate?"

Zoey shrugged. "Probably not. They have online classes at a lot of different schools, but it's hard to keep up with assignments when I'm out here in the middle of nowhere. Just look at how much trouble we're hav-ing contacting the home base right now. It's not usu-ally like that, by the way, but even if the radio worked perfectly every time and I could always have internet access, I would still have trouble finding the time to study. As you're seeing during this trip, it's not your standard eight-to-five gig."

As if to accent the point, they heard a loud splash and yelling up ahead. Zoey's eyes immediately went to the group of kayakers ahead of them, and as the group moved, she could see that John Webster's boat had over-turned and he was flailing in the water. Webster was wearing his life vest, but it was obvious he wasn't a very good swimmer. It wasn't helping that Lucas was nearby, pushing him under with the tip of his paddle, and that others who were in the same vicinity were cheering him on.

A cold fear gripped Zoey as she moved as quickly as possible to reach the group. Were they really going to kill the man and sentence him to death without any proof that he was the murderer? Hadn't they just gone over this a short time ago? She remembered reading *Lord of the Flies* by William Golding back in her high school days. The story of kids turning on each other had seemed far-fetched to her then, but that was back when she was still an innocent kid and hadn't seen how ugly some people could treat each other. She'd seen a lot of spitefulness and malice since then. How was she going to stop these campers from turning on one of their own?

SIX

"Leave him alone!" Zoey demanded forcefully, her tone loud and full of authority.

As Josiah watched, she rammed Lucas's kayak with her own near the rear starboard section, and there was a large smash of rotomolded polyethylene as the two boats collided. She had moved so quickly Lucas hadn't even had time to react. Neither kayak was damaged, but as the material flexed and bent, the impact turned Lucas's boat around and sent him several feet away toward the shoreline. He said something angry under his breath but didn't challenge her. Zoey got closer to Webster and reached out her paddle to him in the water so he could hold on to one end and catch his breath. He was wearing his dry suit and a life vest, like everyone, and had only been bobbing in the water for a couple of minutes, but his face was red—either from exertion or humiliation, Josiah wasn't sure which. He sputtered and treaded water, his hands holding tightly to her paddle as he regained his breath and energy.

"We just had this discussion a few minutes ago," Zoey said tightly. "I realize everyone is stressed, but we can't afford to turn on one another. Mr. Webster, like all of you, is innocent until proven guilty. You *will* leave him alone from this point forward. In fact, Mr. Quinn, the owner of this tour company, will be personally protecting him. If anyone tries to hurt Mr. Webster again, we'll make sure law enforcement brings charges for assault and battery against that individual, or every single one of you in the group—" she glared at Lucas and Mia "—as soon as we reach the base camp."

She glanced over at Josiah, and he nodded his agreement. After their last discussion, he was determined to support her and let her lead, as promised. She was the expert here, and she did need them to respect her leadership. If they questioned her at every step, someone could definitely end up getting hurt, and that was the last thing he wanted. It was hard for him to sit back and watch as someone else took command, but maybe God was trying to teach him something. If he was going to keep Zoey on as the guide for these trips, which he had already decided to do, then they needed to learn how to work together. Hopefully, now that she knew her job was safe, she would feel a bit more at ease around him. Josiah knew his father had rarely gotten involved in any aspect of the Tikaani tours, and he was beginning to understand why. Zoey was more than capable. She was a talented and dynamic leader. Still, he wanted to have some role in this company, and he wasn't used to sitting on the sidelines while someone else took the lead. It was obvious that Zoey was also used to doing everything all by herself. Maybe, just maybe, they could decide the best path forward as a team. Josiah was willing to bend—up to a point. Would Zoey be flexible, too?

He kept a wary eye on the others as Zoey left Webster with her paddle and jumped into the water. Then she swam up next to his kayak, pulled herself up on top of the flipped boat and grabbed the handle of the opposite side. She rocked a couple of times but was then able to flip it back over by using her weight to pull it upright. Thankfully, all of Webster's equipment was securely tied down and still in the kayak, or he would have lost his tent, food and other supplies.

She held his kayak firmly near the front of the boat while still treading water. "Okay, Webster. Go ahead and get back in."

He nodded at her, pushed her paddle toward Josiah and pulled himself back in the boat. His whole body was shaking, and it was obvious that the experience had truly traumatized him.

Once he was seated again and ready to go, Zoey returned to her own kayak and pulled herself back into the seat while Josiah held it steady for her and returned her paddle. The others lingered and watched, mostly with expressions of disgust or anger.

"You're protecting a murderer, you know," Mia accused, her tone acerbic. "He'll kill us all, one by one, if we don't stop him."

"You don't know that," Zoey returned. "If you have some proof you'd like to share with me, I'd be happy to see it. Otherwise, you'll stay away from Mr. Webster."

Josiah gripped the side of his kayak, trying hard to stay quiet. He let her lead but brought his boat up next to hers, silently giving her his support and showing the group that he had her back. Zoey could handle this. In fact, her next words made it apparent to him that she was trying her best to smooth over the incident and get everyone back on the right track.

"Look, I realize this situation is stressful and everyone is scared. All I ask is that we try not to speculate and accuse someone without proof. We'll be down the mountain in no time and can let law enforcement take over. I'm sure they will do a thorough investigation and discover the identity of the guilty party."

Patricia shook her head, seemingly unconvinced. "You probably didn't hear him, but Webster just confessed that he killed poor Mr. Garcia right before you joined us. He as much as admitted they were both embezzling funds from the company and Mr. Garcia had gotten greedy and taken the lion's share of the stolen money."

"I did not," Webster sputtered. "I said that *I* suspected Marty Garcia of embezzlement. I never said that I participated. I would never do that. To be completely honest, that's what we were arguing about the night before he died. You know I work in the purchasing department. I saw some orders that didn't make sense and some other irregularities that have been going on for a few months. I confronted him, but he denied having any knowledge of the problems. That was the end of it. I promise I had nothing to do with his death. I *did not* murder that man."

"It sure is interesting how your story changes the minute Zoey and Josiah come along." Patricia sneered.

"Maybe you can convince them, but you can't convince me! You're out to save your own neck."

"Enough!" Zoey exclaimed. "Patricia, go on down the river, please."

The faces of the other campers now ranged from incredulousness to outright disbelief, but still no one spoke up against Zoey or said anything further. Josiah's muscles were tense and ready to spring into action if needed, but apparently the group as a whole decided to move along without further discussion. Some muttered under their breath, but they once again slowly dispersed.

"Stay with us," Josiah suggested as he caught Webster's eye. "I don't want them to get you alone again like that."

Webster nodded. "I guess I have to. They're so filled with fear and suspicion, not one of them can even hold a normal conversation. I'm scared to even be around them."

"I'm sorry they're being so difficult," Zoey said. "We've only got about another half an hour on the river or so. Then we'll stop for dinner and set up our camp for the night." She straightened her boat and the three of them followed after the rest of the campers. "Hopefully they'll start to see reason before too long. But if they don't, remember to stick close to Josiah."

Webster glanced over at Josiah. "Will you really help me if they turn against me again?"

"I will," Josiah confirmed. "Just as Zoey said—everyone, including you, is innocent until proven guilty. I'm going to let law enforcement sort it out." Webster looked relieved as they started to paddle down the river, but his face looked gaunt and showed the stress and strain of the day. Even his eyes were watery and rimmed in red. Josiah wasn't 100 percent convinced of the man's innocence, but he would protect him anyway, guilty or not. Josiah didn't want Webster hurt because the others wanted to play judge, jury and executioner all in one fell swoop. He hoped it wouldn't come to a showdown before this trip concluded, but he would do whatever he could to keep anyone else from getting hurt.

He watched as the man's hands shook, even as he slowly paddled. What if he was guilty and just very, very good at hiding it? Josiah wondered. Would he or the real killer try to kill again? Were any of them safe?

After about ten minutes, Zoey left Josiah with Webster and moved to the front of the group so she could encourage them again and get a feel for their overall mood. She went over the instructions for the next leg of the trip and asked them to keep an eye out for bears with their cubs, which could sometimes be seen along the rocky shoreline. She hoped that focusing on the beauty that surrounded them might be a positive distraction, so she pointed out interesting flora and other wildlife that they also might see along the way. The horrible stress that had been so evident among the group only a few minutes before seemed to have dissipated somewhat, but she could still feel a tension in the air, especially when she looked at the stormy expressions on Mia's and Lucas's faces. Still, they didn't challenge her or cause further problems.

About half an hour later, having followed Zoey's deft

lead, they arrived at their next campground, which was a flat, sandy area next to the river that offered a beautiful view of the nearby mountains and forest. The river curled around the terrain in shades of light green and blue, adding even more beauty to the scene, and the sun was lower on the horizon and sent a soft light through the canopy of trees. Alaska in May was a wonderful sight. The air was fresh with new beginnings, and even though it was a little bit cooler than in the later months, the landscape was already alive as plants and flowers budded and set the stage for wildlife sightings. Even though the sun set late in May, once June came along, it would never truly get dark in the evenings, and campers usually experienced eighteen hours of sunlight each day well into July.

Zoey helped the campers get their kayaks out of the water and then get their tents set up. While Tikaani owned the lakeside land and cabins that the campers used when they started this trip, those buildings were luxuries they'd left behind when they headed down the river. Now each person or couple carried their own tent and supplies, as well as part of the group's food supplies, on their own kayak. The group was subdued as they set things up and did most of the work silently as they listened to and followed her instructions. She made sure Webster's tent was set up between hers and Josiah's, and all of the tents circled a pile of rocks that had obviously been used as a firepit in the past by previous groups. Then she gave the group a quick fly-fishing lesson and sent them back to the river, asking them to spread out to give each person some space. Only a few wanted to fish, but all of them seemed to want to be away from Webster, who also opted out. He changed into his camp clothing and then decided to gather materials for the fire. He promised to stay within eyesight in case he was ambushed again and walked around the perimeter of the campground picking up sticks and small logs.

Zoey inhaled deeply as she watched the campers disperse around the river. She had also changed out of her dry suit and was feeling very comfortable in her lined hiking pants and flannel shirt. In May, they hoped for highs in the fifties, and today felt warmer than most, even though there was still snow on the ground higher on the ridges. The air was moist, as if rain was coming, and mist rose above the river water, giving the land a surreal appearance. She never got tired of looking at the beautiful scenery or hearing the frogs or other animals that welcomed them to the area. Still, their current circumstances put a damper on the trip, and for the first time ever, she was anxious to complete this expedition and return to the base camp so law enforcement could do their jobs and ferret out the killer. She said a short and silent prayer, asking God to give her strength to make it through the days ahead and to protect Webster during the rest of the trip.

When she finished, she walked into the woods, leaving the group behind her, and Webster in Josiah's hands so she could try the handheld radio again in private. She was still unable to reach the base camp, and frustration filled her, despite her serene surroundings. When were they going to be able to communicate again with the outside world in a meaningful way? A measly 160 characters didn't allow for much of a conversation, yet that was all the radio would allow. She felt very isolated and alone, despite the group of people nearby that were depending on her to get them to safety.

The fear of the killer among them brought back memories of the anxiety she had felt back when she had been dating her abusive boyfriend, and a sharp pain twisted in her stomach, reminding her of the physical and mental anguish the man had caused. She didn't want to think about him ever again, but his face appeared in her mind's eye, and she couldn't seem to rid herself of the image, no matter how hard she tried. His deep-set, dark eyes were the worst. Most of the time, they had followed her every movement, analyzing, finding fault and seeking to control her actions. She didn't want to remember him or the pain he had caused. Looking back, she knew she had stayed with him way too long, but it had been hard to pull away, and he had constantly threatened to come find her if she ever tried to escape. Fortunately, he had been arrested and was now serving time for tax evasion in a minimum-security prison in California. His arrest had given her the break she'd needed to disappear from his life and start anew. She'd been living in Alaska, leading these expeditions, ever since.

She returned to the campground and watched as some of the campers playfully skipped rocks across the water. She was glad they were able to relax a little, and she hoped this evening would go smoother than the day had gone. The river had been running a bit fast for the last hour, and it had taken some level of concentration to navigate it. Hopefully, that exertion had refocused the group and taken their interest away from convicting Webster. She hoped they would have a calm night—free from accusations and fear.

"Any luck with the radio?" Josiah asked. He was sitting on a large boulder, watching Webster build the fire with birch bark and pine needles, and whittling a small piece of wood with a pocketknife. It had been challenging for Webster to find enough dry materials to even start a fire since it was so humid outside, but the tinder was dry, and he had found a few dry logs buried beneath wetter ones, so he was actually able to get a small blaze going, despite the moist air. He waved to Josiah as he wandered toward the trees out of earshot, to look for more wood, but still within eyesight.

Zoey watched him carefully, then turned her attention back to Josiah. "Nope. Still just static. I sent in our location, so at least they know we're on the move. They responded via text on the high frequency handheld radio and confirmed a storm is still causing interference." She watched his hands as they deftly carved on the wood. "Is that Alaskan birch wood?"

"Yep," he replied. "This piece has a beautiful color to it, don't you think?" He moved it slightly and the light-colored wood gave way to a ring of darker brown that decorated the longer side. She'd seen a few people whittle along these trips and enjoyed seeing what could be done with just a simple piece of wood. She had no artistic ability at all and admired those who did. Even if the final product was less than perfect, she was sure he was doing a better job than she could do.

"Yes, I like it. What are you making?" He was still in the beginning stages, and she didn't want to hurt his feelings by guessing incorrectly.

"You can't tell?" he asked, but there was a smile in his voice that he was trying to hide.

Oh boy. Now she was in trouble. She tilted her head to the side, considering the piece of wood that really didn't have much shape to it yet. "Well, I'm guessing something aquatic." She hedged. She had a fifty-fifty chance.

"I'm crushed!" he declared, and for a minute, she thought he was serious. Then he grinned at her and gave her a wink.

Oh, what an amazing smile it was! Had he ever smiled at her like that before? It lit up his entire face and made him seem approachable—even friendly. Suddenly the air felt thick, and her knees went weak. Even her heart seemed to be beating harder against her chest. Why was she acting like a young coed around her boss, and why was she noticing his smile in the first place?

Suddenly, understanding dawned. It had been years since she had noticed any man's smile. That's why. The feelings of attraction were so foreign—she hardly recognized them. But was she seriously attracted to Josiah Quinn? The mere thought unnerved her, and small beads of sweat seemed to instantly form on her forehead just at the thought.

He seemed to realize she was discombobulated, but she hoped he hadn't figured out why. He nodded to a nearby part of the rock he was sitting on. "You look like you could use a rest. Why don't you take a seat?"

He worked some more on the wood. "I'll give you a pass on guessing my project for now. It's still early in the game yet."

She exhaled playfully, took his advice and sat on the boulder but left a good distance between them. Sitting for a minute gave her something to do besides think about her crazy reaction to his smile. She was no college girl, and she had toughened up and matured quite a bit since she had left her boyfriend and California behind. She straightened her spine. "Better watch out. If you turn out to be a natural whittler, you'll be forced to start giving lessons to the campers. Look at Lucas over there." She pointed toward Lucas, who was fly-fishing in the river. Every few minutes, he stopped and helped either Mia or Jessie, who both seemed to be struggling with the gear and best technique for casting the line. "He claims he's never gone fly-fishing before, but now he's out there giving lessons."

Josiah laughed. "Good point. I probably don't have to worry, though. I have very little artistic talent. This wood will probably be something completely unidentifiable when I'm finished with it." He did a bit more carving, then suddenly his facial features changed from playful to determined, and he quickly moved toward her with the knife in his hand. His large body loomed over her, and she startled and shrank away from him as if he was about to hit her or use the knife. Fear filled her heart, and a scream felt stuck in her throat.

Was she suddenly in danger from Josiah Quinn?

SEVEN

Zoey's heart slammed against her chest like a jack-hammer, and her hands started shaking. She felt frozen in place even as adrenaline pumped through her veins. Was Josiah Quinn going to stab her?

Josiah raised an eyebrow at her reaction and lifted his hands in mock surrender as he slowly backed away. "Whoa, I apologize. I didn't mean to scare you." He moved even farther back, giving her plenty of space. "Are you okay? There was a large insect coming toward you, and I just didn't want it to bite you. I think they're called 'cow killers' because the sting hurts so much. I just wanted to brush it away. I'm really sorry." He sheathed his knife and secured it in his pocket.

She looked behind her and saw the large offending red-and-black bug scurrying away into a crevice in the rock. It looked like a big hairy ant, but it was actually a form of wasp that had a horrible sting. He had been right to warn her, and she appreciated his help, but she couldn't get past her anxiety, which seemed amplified even more by Garcia's murder. To her chagrin, this latest event had triggered all of her old fears and doubts that she thought she had laid to rest years ago. Her breath was still coming in gasps, but she did her best to steady it.

Her old boyfriend had exerted both physical and emotional abuse on several occasions during their relationship. Would the scars he'd left behind ever heal? Eight years had passed, and she still couldn't handle a man making sudden moves around her. "Sorry. I guess I'm just a bit on edge." The excuse seemed lame, even to her own ears, but she wasn't feeling particularly creative. She glanced up at his eyes, and instead of condemnation, she saw support and interest. She could tell he wanted to know more but wouldn't violate her privacy and ask. There was even a caring look visible in those brown depths—something that said he wouldn't condemn her or tell her that her pain was silly and she should just "get over it," as some of her old friends had done. For the first time in quite a while, she actually felt like sharing.

"I had an abusive boyfriend," she finally admitted. "He beat me on a regular basis, and he was an expert at making sure the marks weren't visible." She grimaced. "Even so, we were together a long time and were about to get married." She sighed and fiddled with a string that was hanging from her cuff. "I guess Garcia's murder has brought back some of those old feelings and fears. The relationship ended several years ago, and it probably shouldn't still bother me, but I just can't help it. It makes me nervous if someone moves too quickly around me. I guess I'm just a bit jumpy."

Josiah slowly and deliberately moved back even further. She appreciated his thoughtfulness.

"I'm sorry to hear that." He tilted his head. "Where is he now?"

"Prison," Zoey said bluntly. "Tax evasion. His arrest actually saved me. I didn't have the strength to pull away from him until that happened."

"You're stronger than you think," Josiah opined.

Zoey shrugged. "I am now. I wasn't then. I've grown up a lot and found myself here in Alaska. I guess that's one reason why I was so concerned about losing my job. I can't really imagine starting over somewhere else. I've finally found the peace and happiness I was searching for, here on this river." She met his eyes again. "Even though I admit that right now I'm a bit jumpy."

Josiah nodded slowly, his expression considering. "I would never hurt you, Zoey. Never. That's just not in my DNA."

She could see the truth of that statement mirrored in his eyes. "I get that," she said softly. "And I believe you. I just can't help my reaction."

He considered her words for a moment. "Okay. Let's make a deal. I'll do my best to move slowly around you and give you the space you need, if you'll be sure to tell me when I'm making you uncomfortable." He drew his lips into a thin line. "I have to admit, I'm not always that conscientious about what others are feeling. The army trained me to complete the mission first and worry about everything else later. I may not know that something I'm doing is bothering you unless you tell me."

Zoey smiled. She was glad he was willing to help

her and be understanding, especially when the hang-ups were hers and hers alone. He was scoring big points in the "friends" department. "That works for me. Deal."

She suddenly felt awkward and needed to escape from this trip down memory lane. She didn't like talking about her past, and embarrassment heated her face. "Time to start dinner. I'll see you later." She stood up and walked toward the river and could feel Josiah's eyes following her. What was he thinking? Had it been wrong for her to admit her problem to her boss?

She tried to push her worries away as she started working with the two campers who were scheduled to make the group's dinner. Everyone on the team rotated assignments, and each took a turn preparing the meal and cleaning up afterward. Because she wanted to keep an eye on him, she pulled Webster in to help as well. The other two were a little standoffish at first, but soon she had the small group working together with a playful banter that helped them get past the awkwardness.

No one had managed to catch a fish, so tonight they were having vegan burritos, and most of the work included chopping vegetables. She found the ingredients in the food bins and went to work. Every few minutes, she glanced over at Josiah, but he was still sitting on the rock, whittling by himself. At times, she saw him verify Webster's safety with his eyes and then return to his wood carving. He reminded her of a sleeping bear. Although he was at rest, she had no doubt he could be up and dangerous in seconds. After all, he was a trained warrior. Even so, the thought actually helped calm her raging emotions. He had said he would never hurt her, and she believed him. In fact, after their short conversation, she actually was starting to feel safe around him. Was that a mistake? Could she trust him?

The meal was uneventful, and Zoey was pleased that the group as a whole had chosen to ignore Webster, rather than continuing their persecution of the man. After cleaning up, most of the group wandered around the campground in pairs or small groups, talking or taking short hikes around the area. It didn't get dark until around 10:00 p.m., but the day had been a long one, and everyone eventually wandered back and headed to their own tents, including Webster. Zoey could see the distress in his eyes, but at least no one else had threatened him or tried to harm him. She could tell Josiah was still keeping watch, and the two of them waited by the fire until everyone was accounted for and in their own tents. Then they each retired to their own tents, leaving the fire burning for warmth and to keep predators at bay.

Zoey had trouble falling asleep, and her mind wandered as she lay in her sleeping bag, looking at the top of her tent but not really seeing it. An hour passed, then another. She was relieved that Josiah had assured her that her job was safe. That had been an unexpected blessing. But she was discomfited about her responses to him in general. One minute she was attracted to him, the next she was terrified of him and the power he exuded. He was a big man, at least six foot one, with broad shoulders and a lean, sleek physique. He had also been a strong military officer who had fought back from a debilitating injury and won the ability to walk again. She'd never had that sort of injury, but she did have

some idea of how hard it must have been for him to recover and fight to regain his physical abilities that the
mortar had stolen from him. She also couldn't deny that
he was doing a good job and she was appreciating his
presence. He had even probably saved her life that first
day when she had been drowning in the bay.

She thought through their various interactions.
His physical strength was only part of the package he
brought to the mix. He had threatened her leadership
but then acquiesced and allowed her to lead. And he had
patiently accepted her odd behavior when he'd brushed
the bug away and given her the space she'd needed to
recover and be able to continue. Maybe he had a softer
side that contained some flexibility, despite his impos-
ing presence.

Could they be friends? Could they work together? It
was hard for her to trust any man, especially one who
was so strong and commanding. Yet she couldn't deny
she was tempted to try. He seemed like someone de-
pendable—someone honorable.

Zoey was so absorbed in her musings that, at first,
she didn't hear the slight scraping sound from outside.
Then a twig snapped, breaking the silence and captur-
ing her attention. She froze, focusing on the noises outside her thin tent walls. She could hear the water rolling
in the river nearby and tumbling over the rocks, but
now she heard something new, as if a person or animal
was walking around the camp. She'd had a bear invade
their campground before and had a can of bear spray
ready. She reached for it and silently wrapped her hand
around the small metal can.

Rocks clinked and shifted. Someone was approaching her tent from behind, and she could make out the sound of their shoes as they walked upon the sandy gravel. Friend or foe? Animal or human? It sure didn't sound like a bear. Then she saw a human silhouette across the top of her tent as the person passed, and she knew for a fact that this was no animal approaching. The person was also carrying some sort of homemade torch, and flames sent shadows scurrying across the tent fabric.

She slowly unzipped her tent, as silently as possible, then pulled herself up to a crouching position at the entrance as the form continued on its trek. Her heart was rapidly beating against her chest, and icy fear swept over her from head to toe. Who was walking around the camp at this time of night, and why were they using a torch instead of a flashlight? Was it the murderer? They had searched through everyone's belongings thoroughly before leaving the base camp, and she knew that no one had a gun on this trip. Even so, there were a lot of other ways to kill a person, and even the rocks from the soil around them could be used as a murder weapon if a person was angry enough to use one.

She tried to steady her breathing as she heard the perpetrator take another step. The offender now seemed closer to Josiah's tent, which was on the other side of Webster's. She wondered fleetingly if either of the two men were awake and heard the person approaching. She glanced at her watch, hit the small light and noticed that it was after midnight. She couldn't count on either of them being awake at this hour.

The perpetrator took another step. Then another.

Suddenly, she made a decision. She wasn't going to be a victim any longer. She was going to fight back and do everything she could to stop whoever was out there before he or she committed another crime and hurt someone else. She mustered her strength, took a deep breath and then surged out of her tent, her flashlight in one hand and the can of bear spray in the other.

"What's going on out here?" she yelled as she emerged, shining her light all around the area. She caught the silhouette of a person standing behind Josiah's tent and pointed her flashlight at the person's face. She smelled a stench that made her nose wrinkle. Was that lighter fluid? The man appeared to stumble, and suddenly, with a *whoosh* sound, Josiah's tent unexpectedly went up in flames.

"Josiah! Your tent is on fire. Josiah!" She immediately closed the distance between her tent and the one that was engulfed in a huge conflagration and cried out in anguish. Was Josiah still inside the tent, about to burn to death?

Lucas Phillips took a step back, his expression obviously surprised at having been caught roaming around the campground. He quickly took off his jacket as Zoey approached and made a show of trying to put out the fire by hitting at the tent with his coat. "Oh no! Help me get the fire out!"

Josiah suddenly appeared from the darkness, and Zoey instantly felt a wave of relief sweep over her. She didn't know why Josiah hadn't been in his tent when the fire had started, but she said a quick prayer of thanks nonetheless. Josiah moved quickly to join Lucas and Zoey as they tried to keep the fire from spreading. Josiah and Lucas beat at the flames with their coats, while Zoey scooped up sand with a bowl she found nearby and threw it on the blaze. Other campers came out of their tents, saw the commotion and disappeared, then reappeared with water in various containers that they threw at the fire. Between their combined efforts, the flames were soon extinguished, leaving a charred mess of burned fabric and bits of the metal frame where Josiah's tent had been only moments earlier. The smell of scorched material filled the air, leaving an acrid scent that permeated the entire campground.

Once the flames were out, Josiah approached Lucas and challenged him, their chests only inches apart. Josiah's tone was caustic and rough. "What were you trying to do, burn me alive?"

"I was just out stretching my legs!" Lucas said defensively. "I'm not used to being in a kayak all day. I couldn't sleep and needed to walk around a bit. I didn't mean to catch your tent on fire. When Zoey called out to me, I dropped the torch I was carrying. I didn't mean any harm, I promise!"

"Oh really?" Zoey said, unable to keep the disbelief from her voice. She glanced around, searching for an accelerant. "Is that why I saw you reaching the torch toward his tent? And what was that smell? Gasoline? Lighter fluid? These tents are chemically treated to resist fire, but you put something on the fabric to make it burn." She took a step closer to him. "You set Josiah's tent on fire to kill him! You're the murderer! And here you were, leading the charge to convict Webster yesterday when it was you all along!"

"I didn't mean to hurt Josiah. This was an accident. I swear!" Lucas yelled back, his tone defensive. "And I didn't kill Garcia. I barely knew the man. Webster is the killer, not me."

"That's not true," Patricia said softly.

Zoey shone her light around the campground and saw several of the other campers who had been drawn out of their tents because of the fracas.

"What do you mean?" Mia said, taking a step toward Patricia. "My husband wouldn't hurt anyone on purpose. If he says it was an accident, then it was an accident. Be careful who you accuse," she spat.

"Maybe," Patricia hedged, "but Lucas knew Marty Garcia was embezzling funds. I know he contacted the board and reported what he found."

"That doesn't mean anything," Jessie said quickly. "The board never took any action against Mr. Garcia."

"Sounds like motive to me," Nolan McAdams said with a tone of sarcasm tinting his voice. Up until now, he'd been one of the quieter campers who had pretty much stayed in the background, but now his eyes glowed with anger. "They wouldn't do anything about the embezzlement, so Lucas must have decided to take the matter into his own hands." He took a few steps toward him. "Is that why you killed Garcia? To pay him back for destroying Western?"

Zoey took a step forward, her light still focused on Lucas. "Maybe revenge was a motive for killing Mr. Garcia, but why would you hurt Josiah? He's not involved with Western's internal problems. It doesn't make any sense."

"I wasn't trying to hurt Josiah," Lucas said stiffly. "I was out. Stretching. My. Legs. I said that already. I got a little lost when I was out walking around and was just trying to find my tent. Then I tripped and dropped the torch." Lucas stood up straighter, daring any of the campers to disagree with him.

Josiah didn't believe the man's claims, but no immediate motive jumped to mind either. Zoey had a point. Why would Lucas want to hurt him? Regardless of the answer, there wasn't much he could do about it at this point anyway. They had a new suspect, but it was the middle of the night, law enforcement was miles away and there was still no proof. He sure was glad he'd had to go to the bathroom, or he could have been severely injured in the fire.

He glanced over at Zoey, who looked even more stressed than she had earlier this evening when they had been talking. He knew she preferred to lead, but this attack had been directed at him, and in his mind, it was his problem to address. He hoped he didn't step on her toes when he took charge of this particular situation.

"Everyone, go back to your tents. You, too, Lucas. I'll stand guard for the rest of the evening and make sure everyone stays safe."

Lucas looked relieved, and Patricia raised her eyebrows as if she was about to argue, but Zoey spoke up from behind him. "Good night, everyone. Get some rest. We have a lot of paddling to do tomorrow."

The group slowly dispersed, and Josiah felt a wave of relief sweep over him. He would have defended himself, if necessary, but he didn't want to cause any more strife within the group, and without proof of some sort, there really wasn't much more he could do about the fire. No real harm had been done, and thankfully, his military days had taught him how to survive with very little sleep. In his mind, it was worth losing a few hours of shut-eye to ensure everyone's safety and make sure nothing else happened during the night.

He made his way over to the campfire, stoked it and made himself comfortable leaning against a nearby rock as the others disappeared back into their tents. He could survive without a sleeping bag and the extra set of clothes that had been in his tent, and thankfully, his backpack was still sitting by the campfire where he had left it earlier in the evening.

Josiah was pleasantly surprised when Zoey came over and joined him a few minutes later, even though she left quite a distance between them. She shrugged when he raised an eyebrow.

"I can't sleep," she said softly. "Not after you could have died or been seriously injured. I know he put something on your tent to make it go up in flames like that. He can claim it was an accident all day long, but that's not what I saw. That fire was deliberately set."

"We just can't prove it," Josiah said. "I feel like we can't trust a single one of them. I guess we'll both be watching our backs until we get these people down the river and back to civilization."

Zoey shifted. "Do you know anything about Western? It sounds like the store is in big financial trouble, and I just wonder if the problems it's having are related to what's going on during this trip."

Josiah jabbed at one of the burning logs. "I'm still trying to get familiar with all of my dad's assets that I inherited on his death, but I can tell you this—even though he used to own a significant portion of their stock, he sold all of his interests in Western a few months ago. I have no idea why, but with all of this talk about embezzlement, I'm not too surprised. If he got a whiff that something improper was going on, I'm sure he would have sold out and focused on his other projects. He had a low tolerance for failure."

Zoey seemed to digest this. "I don't think I ever mentioned how sorry I am about your father's death. When I first started at Tikaani, he let me work in the office to get my feet wet, and then he gradually gave me more and more responsibility. Before I knew it, he had me leading expeditions. I couldn't have done that when I first moved to Alaska, because I was still reeling from everything that happened with my ex-boyfriend. But as I regained my confidence, your dad really encouraged me to get out there and challenge myself. I'll never forget how much he helped me. He was really patient and encouraging."

Josiah was quiet for a moment, thinking of his father. He could see him working with Zoey and helping her recover from the abuse she had endured. Chase Quinn had a habit of challenging people to be the best they could possibly be. At times, Josiah had chafed against the high expectations, but he couldn't argue with the results. He had been a success in the military largely because of his father's training and upbringing.

"I owe a large part of who I am to my dad. But I have to admit, sometimes it's hard to live up to the expectations he set for me. I was his only child, and he was determined to see me succeed in every endeavor. He left huge shoes to fill, and I hope I'm up to the task."

Zoey frowned. "Do you have doubts?"

"I didn't before I got injured." He rubbed his damaged leg thoughtfully. "I've just been struggling since I got hurt. I had my whole future planned out, and now I've got to go down an entirely different path. This is not the future I had envisioned, and I don't do well with change." He sighed. "I guess you could say I'm learning as I go, and I just don't want to let my dad down in the process."

Zoey shook her head. "There's no way you could disappoint him." Her eyes brightened. "Sure, it will take some time to sort everything out, but you'll get it done. If you could tackle learning to walk again, I doubt much else could really slow you down."

He shrugged. "Maybe, but I have to admit, I'm struggling. I don't want to make a mistake. When I got injured, it felt like the sand was shifting underneath my feet, and I still don't feel like I'm on solid ground yet."

He glanced over at Zoey and was relieved to see interest and understanding rather than sympathy. He was glad she was such a good listener. This was the first time he had even expressed these doubts that had been floating around in his mind, and it felt good to finally share these feelings with someone who had understood his father and the taskmaster he had been. His father had been driven—there was no denying it, and Josiah had inherited that same drive. Still, the injury had proved that he could be hurt, and it had shaken his confidence, despite the outward appearances he tried to exude. That mortar fragment that had damaged his leg had also damaged his plans for his entire future, and now he was on a path he had neither chosen nor desired.

Could he be successful in the business world, taking over his father's interests and managing the man's small empire that he had amassed during his lifetime? Was that the life he even wanted?

Josiah was going to have to make some decisions and make them soon. Business managers and owners who had been involved with his father had already been contacting Josiah, asking for directions on how to move forward and seeking his input. Now Josiah just had to decide how he wanted to proceed.

If he lived that long. His thoughts moved to Lucas. The look in the man's eyes had been spiteful and dangerous. Despite Lucas's words, Josiah knew that he would have been severely injured if Zoey hadn't stopped Lucas when she did.

He was beginning to wonder, would any of them actually survive this trip?

EIGHT

The sun rose at about four forty-five in the morning the next day, but Josiah didn't see any movement around the camp until about seven. At that point, people slowly started emerging from their tents one by one, rubbing the sleep from their eyes and stretching as they started their morning routines. He counted them as they all went about their business, and after a few minutes, he concluded that everyone was up and moving. Mia and Jessie were on breakfast duty, and the two of them washed at the river, then came back and started putting together the pancakes, fruit, coffee and tea that would make up the first meal of the day. The others started packing and policing the camp, making sure they would leave no trace behind them after they returned to the river.

During the night, Josiah had switched back and forth between walking around the campground and sitting by the campfire. He hadn't had to pull guard duty in years, and he had to admit, he was a bit tired after all. Those feelings were nothing, however, compared to the relief he felt that everyone had survived the night and nobody else had been hurt or harassed on his watch. In fact, he hadn't seen anything else suspicious or alarming happen since the episode with Lucas late the night before. Hopefully, now that everyone was up and keeping an eye on each other, the killer would refrain from attacking anyone else.

Zoey approached him as he finished his last circuit and handed him a cup of coffee while sipping on her own mug of the steaming brew. "Are you doing okay? You've got to be exhausted." They had talked a bit more at the campfire after the episode with Lucas, but she had eventually gone back to her tent for a bit more sleep. It had been a good conversation, and Josiah enjoyed getting to know her better. They talked a bit about their pasts and various jobs they had worked growing up. Most importantly, she had seemed more relaxed around him, and for that he was grateful. Now she was up and ready to go and had already donned her dark blue dry suit for the day's kayak trip and pulled her dark brown hair back into her normal ponytail. He couldn't help but notice how her hairstyle accented her high cheekbones and wide mouth, and how her dry suit accented her curves in all the right places. When she smiled, she was one of the most beautiful women he had ever seen.

Josiah pushed those thoughts away. Now wasn't the time to be admiring her or thinking about getting to know her better. He needed to stay focused on the campers' safety. "I'm a bit tired, but I'll make it." He took the cup and felt a jolt of electricity shoot up his arm as their fingers touched. His eyes flew to hers to see if she had felt it, too, but all she did was smile. So much for keeping his thoughts away from Zoey. Her blue eyes were

clear and her skin looked fresh and bright. How did she
manage to look so beautiful so early in the morning? He
rubbed his hand absently over the stubble on his chin
as he watched her sip her coffee. Despite his army job
and the early hours his work had required, he'd never
developed into a morning person. Zoey was the opposite. She seemed to glow.

He caught himself on that thought. She was a pretty
woman, but he had no business noticing. His eyes
strayed to her lips as she took another drink, and he
forced himself to look away. So what if she had a lus-
cious, sweet mouth that he was aching to explore? Who
cared if she had beautiful skin that seemed to beg for
his touch? His last relationship had been a disaster, but
for far different reasons than Zoey's former relationship.
His last girlfriend had been the love of his life—that
is, he had believed she was until he discovered she'd
cheated on him while he was on tour in Afghanistan.

He thought back to those pain-filled days and his
brow furrowed. The mistake had definitely been his,
despite his girlfriend's behavior. He'd seen signs that
should have warned him of her unfaithfulness, but he'd
been so enamored with her that he'd either ignored them
or tried to explain them away in his mind. Ever since,
he tried to stay as far away as possible from the fairer
sex. He had enough on his plate right now anyway. The
last thing he needed was a relationship. Zoey was great,
but she was also lugging around a great deal of bag-
gage. It would take someone with exceptional patience
and tenderness to win her over and treat her with the
love and support she deserved. He hoped she would be

able to find that special someone at some point in her life, but it wasn't going to be him.

But if he wasn't interested, why did these feelings of protectiveness and attraction spring up whenever he was around her? He didn't want to experience these emotions, but he couldn't seem to help himself. He tried to push the thoughts away, but it was not an easy task. He didn't even want to consider the possibilities. Thankfully, Nolan approached them at that moment and broke his train of thought, saving him from saying or doing something stupid.

"Have either of you seen Patricia?" he asked, an edge of worry tingeing his voice. "She asked me to help her pack up her tent this morning, but I haven't seen her."

That wasn't good. Josiah felt his chest tighten. He hadn't seen anything suspicious since they'd caught Lucas roaming about, but he was only one man with one set of eyes. He'd also assumed that once the sun was up, the danger had diminished. "She was here a few minutes ago," he said firmly. "I saw her go back in her tent after the excitement last night, and at about seven this morning, she headed out to the woods for a walk. I assumed she was looking for some privacy and would come right back."

Nolan put his hands on his hips. "Well, I don't think she's returned, and I'm worried. Can you help me look for her? It's weird. She really seemed like she wanted my help. I don't think she would have said that if she hadn't meant it."

"I'll help look for her," Zoey said quickly as anxiety started to surge through her veins. "Maybe she just got turned around out in the woods. That happens to the best of us sometimes."

"We'll get the others to help, too," Josiah said crisply. He motioned to get the attention of the five or six people who were standing around the campfire, including Mia, Lucas and Jessie. "Has anyone seen Patricia?"

"Not since midnight," Mia volunteered. "Weren't you guarding the campground?"

Josiah nodded. "Yes, while everyone was sleeping. She went back to her tent and stayed there until everyone got up and started moving about this morning. A few minutes ago, I saw her head into the woods over there." He pointed toward the tree line.

"You let her go into the woods alone?" Jessie said, her voice somewhere between fearful and angry.

"I can keep watch just fine while people are sleeping," Josiah replied. "I can't escort everyone around once they're up. There's only one of me and nine of you."

"So what's the big deal?" Lucas said caustically as he brushed the hair out of his eyes. "She'll return in time for breakfast." He looked at his watch. "She knows we eat at eight. She'll probably turn up any minute. I bet she's out taking a walk and using the facilities."

"No," Nolan said in disagreement. "She wanted me to help her take down her tent and pack everything up. That was about thirty minutes ago. She would have been back by now. I'm sure of it."

More anxiety slid down Zoey's spine. Could Patricia be hurt and out in the forest by herself? "Well, just in case she twisted her ankle or something, let's spread out and see if we can find her. I'd rather be safe than sorry." She pointed toward the path that led into the woods. "Lucas, you and Josiah go that way. Nolan, you head east." She motioned with her hand again. "Mia, you and Jessie please head to the west. I'll follow the river downstream and make sure I don't see any sign of her." She tightened the band on her ponytail in a nervous gesture. "The rest of you, please stay here at the camp and shout out if she returns." Had something happened to Patricia? The woman was an outspoken gossip, but surely no one would hurt her. "I'm sure we'll find her in no time."

The group dispersed, following their assignments, and Zoey was thankful that she'd already donned her dry suit so she could check along the water's edge. She expected one of the campers to find Patricia safe and sound out walking somewhere, but it paid to be prepared for whatever was heading their way, and if she needed to go into the water for any reason, the dry suit was a necessity. On a good day, the water temperature was in the high forties or low fifties. She was convinced her dry suit, and Josiah's quick thinking, had saved her life when she'd nearly drowned in the bay. If he hadn't pulled her out, she might have died from hypothermia. The cold temperatures were a real danger in the Alaskan waters.

She made for the river right by the campground and scanned the water from bank to bank but didn't see anything unusual. The current was flowing pretty fast today, and she made a mental note to mention it to the campers before they launched their kayaks. It wasn't dangerously fast, but different enough from the norm that she would need to caution them before they headed out after breakfast.

She continued walking along the rocky shore, keeping her eyes open for anything that might be a sign of Patricia's whereabouts. Suddenly, she stopped, her eyes riveted on the far bank of the river. A mother moose and her calf were approaching the water from the opposite tree line. The baby was still fairly new and wobbled slightly as it walked. The mama moose came back to the baby's side and nudged it several times, encouraging the tiny calf, until they both made it to the river for a drink. Even though Zoey had seen a similar sight on numerous occasions, she was spellbound. The last few days had been filled with strife and stress, and yet here was a poignant reminder of God's grace and beauty around her.

She stopped and said a prayer of thankfulness as she watched the two magnificent creatures. Even in tough times, God would never abandon her. The beautiful picture playing out in front of her was a gentle reminder. But had she discarded God? When was the last time she had read her Bible or really prayed? Regret filled her. She said another short prayer, this time asking for forgiveness. God needed to come first. Somewhere along the way, there had been a slow fade, and her relationship with God had taken a back seat to the pressures and issues of the day. She took a moment to appreciate the wonder around her, taking in several deep breaths of the cool mountain air. A sense of peace enveloped her, even after the moose and her baby scampered away.

Zoey turned and headed south, following the river.

The wind whispered in the birch trees, and the sand, gravel and leaves crunched under her feet as the water noisily flowed at a hurried pace. She continued about half a mile, then turned as the river made its way around an outcrop of rocks.

That was when she saw the body.

Knots of fear twisted in her stomach as she splashed into the shallow pool formed by the boulders toward the figure. It was the form of a woman, and a sick feeling swept through Zoey's body. The corpse was floating motionless in the water, facedown, and even before she reached it and flipped it over, she could tell it was Patricia. The size and shape matched, as did the dark brown hair and dark green jacket that she'd seen the woman wear. Nearby, a green bandanna that Patricia liked to wear over her hair was tangled in the branches of a dead tree that had fallen into the water. As Zoey got closer, she could see the victim's hands, feet and forehead were dragging against the bottom of the shallow water, and there were fresh abrasions and bruises where the current had pushed her against the rocks in a monotonous motion.

"Help!" Zoey yelled, hoping her voice would bring the others to her location. "I've found Patricia! Help!"

Zoey grabbed the woman's arm and immediately felt for a pulse, but there was none, and Patricia's skin was icy. It was obvious she was dead, but Zoey didn't want to give up until she had at least tried to save her. Adrenaline and foreboding filled her as she pulled Patricia out of the water and onto a nearby grassy area and began CPR. If she had to guess, she thought the poor woman had probably been strangled or drowned. She was no expert, but there were red petechiae dots on the woman's eyes and cheeks, showing that her breath had been restricted, as well as bruising along the woman's neck that resembled a person's handprint.

"Help! I found Patricia!" she yelled again between breaths.

She kept up with the CPR, even as she heard others approaching.

Mia was first on the scene, and when she saw what had happened, she let out a high-pitched wail that curled Zoey's toes. "Oh no! Is she dead?"

Zoey didn't take the time to answer but kept trying to get the woman's heart and breathing restarted. She felt a gentle touch on her arm but pulled away, furiously trying to save Patricia.

"That's enough, Zoey. She's gone." Josiah's soft voice barely penetrated, and she kept going, alternating between compressing the woman's chest and providing the rescue breathing.

She felt the hand return to her arm, and this time, he tugged lightly against her, slowing her motion. She looked up to see Josiah crouching next to her. Compassion filled his features. "You've done all you can. She's dead."

Zoey leaned back, tears in her eyes. He was right. Despite her efforts, Patricia hadn't recovered. She reached over and closed the poor woman's eyelids so she couldn't see the blank stare reflecting back at her. Grief suddenly overwhelmed her. Zoey barely knew the woman, but to die so violently…

Josiah stood and pulled Zoey tenderly into his arms,

and she went willingly, seeking comfort. After a moment, she realized she was allowing his touch, even welcoming it, and the thought surprised her, especially since she'd had such a negative reaction recently when they'd been sitting on the rocks and he'd gotten too close to her. He gave her a bear hug, and for the first time since they'd pulled her from the water after nearly drowning in the bay, she actually felt safe.

More campers quickly arrived on the scene, and she heard murmurs and dismay coming from all directions. Mia and Janey were crying, and Nolan turned on Lucas as soon as he saw Patricia's body and challenged him for all to hear.

"So, when you couldn't kill Josiah, you decided to murder Patricia. Is that what happened?" Nolan pushed Lucas in the chest as he spoke, and Lucas fell back a few steps. Both men were probably in their fifties, but Nolan was a larger man and outweighed Lucas by about fifty pounds. In Zoey's mind, there was no doubt who would win if the two seriously had a battle right there by the river. Lucas fisted his hands and assumed a fighting stance once he regained his balance. His face was mottled with red, but Zoey couldn't tell if it was humiliation or anger that colored his cheeks. "Why would I kill Patricia? I had no beef with her."

"Why would you kill Josiah either? Or Marty Garcia?" Nolan spit out. "I'll leave the 'why' up to law enforcement to solve. All I want to do is survive this trip to Alaska and see that you land in prison where you belong!" He drew back and let his fist fly, just as Josiah released Zoey and stepped in between them.

NINE

Josiah moved Zoey behind him and quickly pushed the two apart and held up his hands as if directing traffic. "That's enough from both of you. Zoey, do you have your cell phone with you?"

"What good is that?" Mia asked scathingly. "It's not like any of us have service out here."

Josiah ignored her as if she hadn't spoken. He met Zoey's eyes. "Do you have it?"

"Yes," Zoey confirmed.

"Okay." He nodded. "Please take pictures of Patricia's body and the surrounding area before the crime scene gets destroyed any further."

He looked around the group that had congregated. They were down to nine including Zoey and himself. No one was missing. "Did anyone see anything? Something suspicious? Someone who wasn't where they were supposed to be?" The group all looked at each other, but no one spoke up, and nobody's body language gave anything away. Yet one of these people standing here was definitely guilty of murdering the poor woman whose body was lying at his feet. Who could have done such a terrible thing? Anger and powerlessness warred for supremacy as Josiah's emotions came bubbling to the surface and adrenaline coursed through his veins. Whoever had done this had probably just been waiting and biding his or her time for an opportunity to catch Patricia alone, and it must have happened just a short time ago. But what could the motive be?

The pain in his injured leg intensified, and it mixed with his frustration. Josiah fisted his hands as restless energy flowed through him. It was all he could do to keep from lashing out at somebody, anybody, until he got the answers he was seeking. Yet he held himself back. Rage wouldn't help the situation. It would just make everything more difficult, and this entire trip was already challenging enough. He took a deep calming breath and motioned to Rick Hall, who was standing off to the side. "Okay, then. Rick, would you help me carry Patricia back to camp after Zoey is finished? Then we'll have to call the base camp again and see where we stand." He sure hoped they could actually reach someone alive on the other end instead of sending another 160-character text. They needed help immediately, but the chances of actually getting the help they needed was slim to nonexistent. One death was scary enough. Having two deaths occur was terrifying. The air felt thick, and he could feel the fear emanating from the other campers. He fully understood why Nolan was in danger of losing his temper and confronting Lucas. If Zoey and the other women weren't present, he probably would have been tempted to do the same, but no matter what, he still couldn't do anything without proof.

Lucas seemed guilty last night of trying to torch Josiah's tent, but what if he wasn't? What if he had been taking an innocent walk and the darkness had made his actions seem more sinister than they really were? Could Lucas have killed Garcia and Patricia both? Or was Webster the murderer and fooling them all? His thoughts churned as he considered the possibilities.

Zoey took several photos and then started herding the others back to camp as Josiah and Rick gently picked up Patricia's body and followed them. He didn't want to move her or destroy the crime scene, but he really had no choice. Wildlife would start swarming the area if they didn't bury her. Their first priority had to be getting the rest of the group back to civilization and safety as soon as possible, including the perpetrator. Josiah knew he was making law enforcement's job harder by trampling the scene, and he said a silent prayer that God would help them discover the murderer's identity before he or she could harm anybody else.

Patricia's body was heavy in his grip, and his heart hurt with the knowledge that this poor woman's life was over for good. He knew very little about her but grieved for her family and friends. Death was so final. He said another prayer, asking God to comfort those who had known and loved her, and also to help him and Zoey keep the peace with the survivors, at least until they could reach civilization again.

Once back at camp, they wrapped her body in a blanket and laid it near her tent, and then Zoey and Josiah walked a short distance away from the group with the handheld radio and tried to reach the home base. It was a dismal failure, and more static was their only response.

Zoey grabbed a nearby rock and threw it harmlessly into the woods. It bounced off a tree trunk and landed with a thud, and she followed it with a second stone. "Ugh! I can't believe I still can't reach them. That must be some horrific storm they're dealing with. It makes me really angry, even though I know it's nobody's fault. I just feel so helpless."

Josiah fisted his hands and looked off into the distance. Somehow, they had to get safely back to the base camp. But how could they do it with a murderer clearly loose among them? "At least let's send another short message, telling them about Patricia's murder. Maybe they can give us some guidance."

Zoey used the keypad and typed, then hit Send and showed Josiah the note on the screen saying the message had been sent. "Okay. Now, what's your best theory about why Patricia was just killed?"

Josiah again thought through the various reasons that might have led to her death. "She worked in the accounting department. My father sold out a while ago, which he wouldn't have done unless the company was no longer a good investment. And there seems to be indications of malfeasance within the company, if Patricia could be believed, which could be why my father sold his shares. Maybe Patricia was wrong about who committed the embezzlement, though, and she was killed to silence her. Or maybe they knew she had saved evidence of the crime and hoped it would never come to light if she died. After all, she seemed pretty bold with her accusations while we were on the river yesterday. Perhaps she said even more to the others and the guilty party got worried that their crime was about to be revealed."

"Makes sense," Zoey said. "But could she have some sort of proof here with her? It seems unlikely. And why would any of this come up during this trip and not before they actually left California, or when they returned? It seems bizarre that all of this is surfacing now, out here in the wilderness."

Josiah nodded. "There's probably more going on here than we realize. That's a big part of the problem—we don't know what we don't know. And without finding some evidence or having someone speak up, there's not much we can do about it out here." He drew his lips into a thin line. "Or maybe the murderer is just choosing his victims at random? I mean, what connection is there between Garcia and Patricia besides the fact that they both work at Western?"

"Well, you also said my near-drowning experience was suspicious, and Lucas definitely seemed like he was trying to hurt you last night when he set fire to your tent. Neither of us has anything to do with Western Office Supply, right? I mean, what's the connection there? None of this makes sense, yet we were targeted as well."

"You're right," he said. "I just don't see how all of these pieces fit together." He put his hands on his hips. "I do think we should search through Patricia's belongings, though, on the off chance we find something we can use to help us solve this puzzle."

"Okay, let's do it." The two went back to Patricia's tent, and after taking pictures of everything, they started sorting through the various items. There wasn't a lot to go through, especially since everyone had to carry their own supplies and one container of food for the group. Space was limited on their kayaks. Josiah set the plastic bear bin with Patricia's share of the food items outside the tent door so they could divide the contents and make sure the food went with them. He motioned to the remaining items, including her backpack, sleeping bag and small red camp pillow. "What's the best way to get all of this other stuff back to the home base?"

"Well, since you need a new tent and sleeping bag, you might as well use hers, but we'll have to leave the kayak and backpack here," Zoey responded. "There just isn't enough room on the kayaks to carry another bag, and the river runs too fast to try to navigate the water and bring the extra kayak back with us. It would be too dangerous to tie it to one of the other kayaks. It's not a big deal, though. Two people from Tikaani can come back and get everything on a separate trip. Whoever comes can start with a tandem two-seater in the bay, and then one person can get Patricia's kayak and paddle it home while the other puts her belongings in the second seat in the tandem kayak to help balance out the weight."

"Sounds good." Josiah picked up Patricia's backpack and sorted through the contents. It had the usual—some toiletries, clothing, a flashlight and two paperback novels. He opened the outside pockets and searched those as well but didn't come up with anything else interesting besides a few personal items. "I'm not finding any clues. Are you?" He looked up and noticed that Zoey had found a small notebook. It had a dark blue cover and was about the size of his hand. The pages were wide ruled and had some sort of writing inside. "Where was that?"

Zoey thumbed through a few of the pages. "I found this notebook in the inner pocket of her jacket. It's got her name inside the cover, but that's all I can read. If memory serves, the rest of this is written in shorthand." She handed him the book. "Does any of that make sense to you?"

Josiah took the book and thumbed through the pages. There were marks on most of them, but they looked like scribbles to him. "Not to me—I don't understand shorthand. We'll have to take this with us to see if we can find someone who can read it."

He watched as Zoey continued the search and found Patricia's phone in another jacket pocket. She pulled it out and offered it to him. "Can you open this?"

He took it and powered it on, but when he swiped it, the numbered keypad appeared. Without knowing the combination, there wasn't much he could do. "Nope. It's password protected like most phones. I didn't know her well enough to even guess at a passcode."

Zoey tilted her head. "I guess we should take both of these items with us for safekeeping. I'm sure law enforcement will want to see both of them as part of their investigation. Maybe they can get inside her phone somehow."

"Agreed."

Zoey looked around the rest of the tent. "There's not much else here—nothing that points to her murder anyway." As Josiah watched, she felt around the woman's sleeping bag roll and pillow but didn't seem to find anything new. Finally, she looked up and caught his eyes. "Looks like we're coming up empty. Any other theories, now that we've searched her things?"

"None," Josiah replied, struggling to keep the disappointment from his voice. "No smoking gun, at any rate."

"I think it's time we had a group meeting. We'll need to tell people what we've discovered or else the conjecture might get out of hand." Zoey lifted her chin. "They also need to know why we never turned back and kept heading down the river without any assistance. Honesty will help keep everyone from guessing."

"All right, let's get them together during breakfast. It should be ready by now anyway," Josiah said. He didn't relish the upcoming conversation. Tempers were running high, and with good reason. What he didn't want was the mob mentality to take over and have the group injure anyone—especially the wrong person. He watched with a guarded eye as Zoey packed up the remains of the items in the tent and made a small pile by the front tent flap. One thing he knew for sure—he was going to do everything in his power to keep Zoey safe. He didn't normally feel such protectiveness toward someone, but there was something about her, something vulnerable and appealing, that touched his heart, broke through the ice that surrounded it and made him want to guard her at all costs. It was a strange feeling, and he didn't welcome it, but as each moment passed, the feeling only seemed to grow within him.

* * *

"We've tried several times to contact the home base, but we haven't been able to reach anyone," Zoey said to the circle of campers as she finished bringing everyone up to speed about their current predicament.

"So no one even knows we're out here dealing with a murderer?" Janey said, her voice incredulous.

"They are aware," Zoey responded, trying to keep her voice modulated and under control. Leadership was important here. "We've been unable to have a voice conversation, but I have been messaging them with our handheld radio. They have been told about both deaths and of our current location via GPS. They are monitoring our progress and have confirmed that our best course of action is to continue on our trek until we reach the Nuka campsite."

"Well, why don't they just fly out here and pull us out of this?" Nolan asked roughly.

"The reason why communication has been so difficult is because of a storm. I'm sure that same storm is making travel difficult."

Zoey motioned with her hands. "But rest assured, the home base is in touch with law enforcement, and the police do know what is going on. As I said, they've given us instructions to continue on to the Nuka campsite, and the police will meet us there. Meanwhile, they have started an investigation."

"How far away is this Nuka site?" Mia asked.

"It should take us two more days to reach it," Zoey responded.

"Two more days? Are you kidding? We could all be dead by then!" Janey said forcefully.

"Webster is the one who murdered Patricia," Lucas said flatly. "And he killed Marty Garcia. If we leave him here, the rest of us will be safe. Let law enforcement come and get him after the rest of us make it down the river."

Rick Hall had been sitting by the campfire, but he suddenly stood, waving his arms around as he talked. "Webster is probably innocent. It's *you* we should be worried about. You probably killed Marty Garcia and Patricia. Don't forget, you're the one we caught trying to set fire to Josiah's tent. And I'd like to know why, right here and right now."

Lucas stood, too, and puffed out his chest as he talked. A moment later, Rick responded in kind. Their actions made Zoey think of two roosters strutting around a farmyard right before they attacked and fought for supremacy. "I was innocently out stretching my legs," Lucas declared. "I've told you that before, and I'm getting pretty tired of repeating myself. I never tried to hurt Josiah."

Zoey put her hands up and was about to try to placate them when Josiah moved in front of her. "What if you're both wrong? The bottom line is, none of us know who the murderer is, and none of us are qualified investigators."

"You don't have to be a rocket scientist to know who killed Patricia!" Rick declared. "It was Lucas!"

"No, it was Webster," Lucas shot back. "I'm innocent. If any of you want to survive this trip, I'm telling you, we need to leave him behind."

"I say leave them both here and let them fight it out," Nolan declared.

"No!" Mia shouted. "You're not leaving my husband out here to die. That's crazy."

Now everyone was on their feet, glaring at one another with mayhem in their eyes. Zoey was suddenly worried that a crowd mentality was about to erupt and even more of them would get hurt. "Enough!" she said, forcefully stepping between Nolan and Lucas. She saw Josiah fist his hands and take a step in her direction, but she sent him a look, letting him know she could handle this discussion without his interference. He'd already stepped in front of her once. She did not want him doing it a second time. This was her problem. She would defuse it right here and now. "Nobody is getting left behind. This is Alaska, and we're deep in the backcountry. It's not safe for anyone to be out here alone who isn't trained in survival skills. That's final, and it's not up for debate." She furrowed her brow. "This is the plan going forward, so everyone needs to get on board. We're going to bury Patricia and leave her kayak and belongings here until we can return sometime in the future and get them. Once we're done, we're going to get in our kayaks and head to the Nuka campsite. That means everyone." She paused and motioned with her hands toward the river. "Rick, I need you and Janey to go get Patricia's kayak and bring it up here to the campground. Then load her belongings in the compartments and make sure everything is closed tightly and as secure as possible." She motioned toward the others. "Lucas and Mia, clean up the breakfast dishes and divide out

Patricia's food that she was carrying to the other bear bins. Everyone else, pack up the camp. I want to be back on the river in thirty minutes."

"Why should we listen to you?" Lucas challenged. "People are dying on your watch. For all we know, you're the murderer."

Zoey narrowed her eyes. "If you want to find your way back to Anchorage by yourself, be my guest, but I'm done listening to your baseless accusations." She pointed toward the tree line. "That direction is south. If you start walking now, you might just make it in a few weeks, if you avoid the grizzlies and wolves, and figure out how to eat off the land without swallowing something poisonous." She kept her voice soft and free from a challenge of any kind. "For those that want to make it back alive to civilization and the base camp, as I said, we'll be leaving in about thirty minutes." She turned and walked back to her tent and started packing, ignoring the stares and looks that followed her. The rest of the group was silent for a few moments, then slowly they dispersed and went about their business. Everyone knew what to do but were moving slower than normal, no doubt still stunned by the news of Patricia's death and the anxiety and stress that plagued the group.

"I thought they'd be a bit more pleased that we have help waiting at Nuka," Josiah said quietly as he came up behind her.

"They're just scared," she replied. "And they have good reason to be." She leaned closer, making sure no one else could overhear them. "Do you have Patricia's notebook?"

"Yes," he said softly. "And her phone, too. I have them wrapped in plastic in the inside pocket of my jacket. I'll keep them with me and turn them over to law enforcement as soon as we arrive at Nuka."

She lifted her chin and caught his eye. "Do you think Lucas was really trying to kill you last night? I mean, it sure looked that way, but why would he want to do such a thing? I just can't figure this out."

Josiah shrugged. "I really have no idea. I've never met him before this trip. I don't see how he would gain anything by my death. What possible motive could he have?"

She rubbed her arms thoughtfully. "Maybe he thinks you know something you don't about Western Office Supply and how it was being managed. After all, money seems to be at the heart of the problem."

"Anything is possible," Josiah said. "But if my father had concerns, he never shared them with me. I don't know a thing about Western." A look of frustration swept over his features and Zoey wondered about the cause.

"Did you just remember something?"

"It's not that," he said firmly. "I just wish I'd done more when my father tried to interest me in his businesses. Before he died, he offered to help me get my feet wet—he wanted me to get more involved. But I didn't. I wasted the opportunity. And now he's gone, and I'll never have that chance again."

She frowned. "But weren't you in the army, serving our country full-time? Weren't you even in Afghanistan on several occasions?"

"Yes. I did three tours. But that's no excuse, and it doesn't take away the regret I feel."

His posture was unexpectedly rigid, as if he was suddenly strung so tightly, he would break with the slightest provocation. Zoey wondered at the cause. She figured it was normal for him to have some remorse after his father died. Didn't everyone want more time with a loved one before death separated them forever on earth? Still, Josiah's reaction seemed a bit strange, and she wondered if there was more to it that he wasn't revealing. She'd known Chase Quinn for years. Now that he was dead, she tried to remember only the good times, but working with Chase hadn't been all puppies and rainbows. There was no room for error, and the man had possessed a quick temper. He had been a good mentor, but he had also been a driving taskmaster, and she suddenly started thinking that Chase might have been even harder on his son than he'd been on her. Had Chase's behavior alienated his son? Or did Josiah feel like he had failed his father in some way? Was Josiah feeling more than the normal regret that came with the finality of death? She wasn't sure, but she hoped her next words would comfort him. "Your army responsibilities sound like a good reason to me. There are only so many hours in the day, Josiah, and it seems like your career kept you pretty busy. I don't know how anyone could have done more."

"The army was demanding, but so was my father. He wanted me to be more involved, but I never listened, and I purposely avoided his demands. And now I'm paying for my lack of foresight. I should have learned all I

could about each one of his businesses so when the time
came for me to take the reins, I would be ready. Well,
the time has come, and I don't have a clue about Western's history or any details that could explain all of this."

"How could you possibly know?" Zoey said, trying
to keep the incredulous tone out of her voice. "You said
yourself Chase sold his shares in the company months
ago."

"If I were half the man my father was, I would have
figured out a way. Sometimes, I think I'm not worthy
enough to manage his companies."

Zoey shook her head. "I don't see how you could
have done more than you did. Weren't you also injured?
And didn't the doctors say you'd never walk again?
Good grief! Give yourself a break! You're not Super-
man, no matter how hard you might have tried. Look at
how far you've come!" She rested her hand on his arm
and gave it a gentle squeeze. "I knew your father—better than most. He was incredibly successful, but he also
never seemed to be satisfied. To him, good was never
quite good enough." She turned so she could meet his
eyes. "He pushed me to be the best I could be, but honestly, I was a project to him, nothing more. He wanted
to prove that he could help me turn my life around, and
he did, and for that, I'll always be grateful. But there
was also a side of your father that was quick to find
fault. Sometimes, he pushed too hard, and if he didn't
get the results he wanted, he would cut bait and turn
to a new project without batting an eye. Believe me,
sometimes he left quite a mess in his wake." She tilted
her head. "It's entirely possible that he stepped on some

toes at Western. Since the company is heading toward bankruptcy, he must have known there were financial discrepancies. Those kinds of issues don't just occur overnight. Yet instead of buckling down and fixing the problems, it sounds like he might have pulled out and left them for others to solve. He took away his money and decided to spend it elsewhere, leaving the concerns to fester and grow." She squeezed his arm again and then took a step closer. "You're twice the man your father was. I think you've done amazingly well. I have some idea of how hard it must have been to overcome your injuries and walk again. And you did it. That alone took a strength of character that I'm not sure your father ever exhibited. You have even more to be proud of. You were an officer in the United States Army. You commanded men and protected our nation. Not to mention the fact that you are here, now, diving in and considering new possibilities for your future as you decide how best to handle your father's estate."

She couldn't quite read Josiah's expression, and she wondered if she'd gone too far in both her condemnation of his father's actions and with her praise of Josiah himself. She searched his eyes and watched his body language, looking for clues, but she really couldn't tell how he had received her words. She'd wanted to encourage him, but her opinions about his father might not have been too well received. Still, she wouldn't regret speaking the truth. She had never been one to beat around the bush or try for subtle hints—she preferred the direct approach. But had she just alienated him for the rest of the trip?

TEN

Later that afternoon, Josiah paddled up beside Zoey, still chewing on the words she had spoken to him that morning. They hadn't had much of a chance to talk earlier because they had been too busy burying Patricia, breaking camp and keeping the various campers' tempers on simmer, but finally they were on the water and heading toward the Nuka camp. Just keeping Lucas and Webster apart had been a major challenge. The two men had been literally at each other's throats, and Josiah had physically had to separate them at one point as they had pointed fingers and blame at each other and traded insults.

The day was overcast, and gray clouds rolled through, bringing rain and mist that surrounded them as they traveled. He watched Zoey slice the water with her paddle and for a moment was swept away by the sheer tranquility of the setting. Beauty was all around them, despite the violence that had marred the trip, and she seemed to have found her niche in life here among the tall, rugged mountains and the cold, winding river. She fit in perfectly. He hoped he could find his own future as she had found hers. His plans were in such an uproar right now that it was hard to even picture where he would be in six months. He longed to return to the life he had known in the army, even though he knew it was an impossibility.

Zoey was beautiful. There was no other way to describe her. She wore no makeup, but her skin glowed with life, and her eyes mirrored her thoughts and animated her face in such a way that he never thought he would tire of looking at her. She had her brown hair French braided today, and he liked the way the style accented her face. Her love of sports had left her body toned, and her motions were smooth and seemed almost effortless. She was strong, despite her past abuse, both physically and emotionally. He wondered if she recognized those strengths, and if she had always been strong, or if her history of abuse had forced her to develop her fortitude and resilience.

He thought back to her words of encouragement again. He was glad she felt confident enough to speak her mind, and he admired the trait. In fact, the last thing he wanted was to try to guess her feelings or motives as they worked together. With Zoey, what he saw was what he got, and he liked that. In fact, compared to his relationship with his old girlfriend, he found Zoey's behavior incredibly refreshing.

But was she right in her assessment? Had his father seen problems at Western and run, rather than staying to fix them? Was there a flaw in Chase and his business acumen that Josiah refused to acknowledge? The picture Zoey painted was difficult for him to take in, and yet some small part of him recognized that the man he had idolized all of his life was not so perfect after all. Memories returned from various situations he had experienced with his father that he seemed to have glossed over, and now he was considering the man and some of those situations with entirely new eyes. According to Chase, his mother had abandoned both him and her son when Josiah was young because she had fallen in love with another. Josiah had only been six at the time and didn't have many memories of the woman. But had she really been unfaithful, or had his father driven her away with his constant criticism and obsessive-compulsive behavior? The answer to that question had never mattered before, but now he wondered and was tempted to see the past with fresh insight and a whole new set of questions. Yes, Chase was a successful businessman, but at what cost? And had Josiah repeated his father's conduct without realizing it and driven his girlfriend into the arms of another? He thought back, considering some of the arguments he'd had with her and the problems they'd had with their relationship. Had Josiah been subconsciously staying away from Chase these last few years as a way to protect himself from the criticism and censure his father so often sent his way? He had to admit, he'd definitely avoided contact. He didn't want to believe these thoughts were true, yet Zoey's words had struck a nerve.

Had Chase been to blame for some of the problems at Western? Did his father really "cut bait and run" when the going got tough, or was he just a smart businessman who knew when it was time to cut his losses and invest in other opportunities that had a better chance of success?

The only way Josiah could really find the answers to his questions was to learn more about his father and his business dealings. But since his father was no longer around to ask, the next best method was to learn as much as he could from those he left behind, and Zoey was right here with him. While he did want to learn more about how Chase operated his businesses, he also wanted to concentrate on just about anything besides Garcia's and Patricia's murders. He had resolved to pick Zoey's brain at the first opportunity, and now that things had settled down and they were kayaking again, it was as good a chance as any.

"Can you tell me more about how Tikaani works? I mean, the tours obviously can't run year-round because of the weather, right?"

"That's right. The early birds start around the first of May, and then the tourist season really gets going around the middle of June and runs until mid-August or so. Near the end of the season in September, the weather gets more unpredictable, and we have to shorten the trips or allow for a great deal of flexibility. By October, it's just too cold to go out and the days are too short to do much anyway."

"What do you do for the rest of the year, then?" Josiah asked.

She shrugged. "I usually teach a couple of online classes at the local community college. I got my bachelor's degree in history, and when I moved up here, I made it a priority to learn about the community and the state in general. Alaska has a rich and vibrant past that

I want to make sure the students understand, so sometimes I teach a class or two in that area. I got my master's in English, though, so mostly that's what I teach. You'd be surprised how many of my students struggle with writing a simple essay." She gave him a small smile. "The bottom line is that I basically just help out where I'm needed. A lot of people leave Alaska during the winter months and work somewhere in the lower forty-eight during the off-season, but I never wanted to go back down there. Alaska is my home year-round, so I just basically hole up during the winter months and teach via my computer."

Based on her history she'd shared with him, he wasn't too surprised about her desire to stay in Alaska, but he was surprised that she was just now mentioning her teaching abilities. It was a new side of her that made complete sense now that she'd revealed it. She was a born leader and educator, and even during this stress-filled trip, she had been teaching her charges a variety of outdoor skills and an appreciation for the land and wildlife around them as they went along. It seemed to come naturally to her.

He pushed his thoughts back to Tikaani. "So how does the company stay solvent with only a few months of business each year?"

"It's not easy. We rent the boat that brought us out here, which is another reason why they couldn't just turn around and come back to get us when Mr. Garcia died. Tikaani is only one of the boat owner's many clients. I maintain the kayak equipment and do the scheduling and most of the purchasing when we need supplies. We have three guides that lead expeditions of various levels of difficulty and in different local areas, and if we're not out on the river or in the bay, then we rotate and stay at the base camp, monitoring the radio. A new expedition starts each week, weather permitting."

"So Tikaani only has the three full-time employees?"

"That's right." She paddled a bit in silence, then added, "Your dad managed most of it when I first got here, but he bought the business from someone else and never led any of the trips. After a while, he trained me to take over, and by the time he died, he was basically just taking a look at the financial statements each month. I rarely saw him or even heard from him, and he seemed happy as long as we were in the black. I got the impression he was busy with other businesses that needed his attention. For the most part, Tikaani runs pretty smoothly."

"What made you want to go from being a guide to managing the company? Did you plan that from the start?" He tried to keep his tone neutral, but she raised an eyebrow. He hadn't meant to offend her, but perhaps he should have worded his question differently. He felt a pit of jealousy twist in his stomach. His father had constantly asked him to work with him, but he had always been so busy with his army career that he had passed on each opportunity. Yet Zoey had learned from his father and benefited from the experience. If he'd done the same, perhaps he wouldn't feel so much trepidation now about the direction his life was going in.

"No, I never expected to run Tikaani. I just worked hard and stepped up whenever Chase needed help. I guess he saw my potential and thought it was worth his time to train me."

"I'm sure he did," he said with genuine admiration. "You've done a great job." He paddled another stroke. "Do you see any expansion possibilities—I mean, if we hired more guides, could we give more tours? Are the customers out there?"

She shrugged. "We're big on wildlife conservation out here. We could probably do a little more, but we don't want to destroy the river by bringing too many people out on the water either."

"But if we hired more guides and ran more expeditions, there'd be a higher profit. I've only begun to look at the numbers, but it doesn't seem like Tikaani is reaching its full potential."

Her eyes narrowed. "What are you trying to say?"

He considered his words more carefully, seeing again that he'd touched a nerve. "I'm not finding fault, but I did notice that the profit and loss statements aren't stellar for this company, and I was thinking that Tikaani might have some excellent growth possibilities."

"Are you unhappy with my management?"

"No—"

"Is that what you're all about, then? Making money?" she interrupted.

"No. I'm just trying to learn more about Tikaani and how you've been running things."

"It sounds to me like you're second-guessing my decisions. Look, I realize you're the owner now, but I guess we need to get our roles clearly defined so I know exactly where I stand. What exactly do you expect of me? I've been running this company without any interference for the last several years. It's small because we like it that way, not because we can't make it bigger or let opportunities pass us by." She tilted her head. "If you have a different plan, you need to tell me now. It's going to be hard for us to work together if we have different visions for where we want this company to go."

Josiah sighed. Coming from a military background, he knew he could come on a bit strongly sometimes. He backpedaled. "Look, I'm sorry if I offended you. That wasn't my intention, I assure you. I'm just trying to understand the business." Zoey said nothing in response, and Josiah tried again. "My father had high expectations for any enterprise, and you told me that, more often than not, if a company wasn't making great profits, he'd pull out and start something new, or he'd just sell out altogether, like what he did at Western. I'm just trying to wrap my head around Tikaani and how it operates."

"We put conservation first and profits second," she said firmly. 'That's how we operate."

Josiah put up his hands in mock surrender. "Okay, got it." Wow. He had really made a mess of this conversation. "Look, I don't mean to imply that you did anything wrong or that I don't agree with your vision. It's just that my father always had high expectations of me, and I want to prove myself worthy of the tasks he left for me. I can't do that without asking questions and understanding what's going on. I'm sorry if I'm stepping on your toes here. I didn't mean to come on so strongly." He purposefully tried to soften his tone. "To be honest, at this point, I'm not sure if Tikaani will even survive after we return to civilization. Once the press gets a hold of these murders, we'll probably be plagued with a boatload of cancellations, and we might even go under." He pushed on. "But regardless of what happens, I want to go on record here and now. I am amazed at your skills and abilities, and the way you've been running the business. You've been doing a great job, and I really don't have any complaints. I'm honestly just trying to understand how it all operates."

Zoey seemed to take this in stride. He met her eyes, and the fire he saw there diminished slightly at his apology. Wow, she was truly alluring, even when she was angry and defensive. He didn't want to feel attracted to her. He didn't want to have this protectiveness surging within him, but he had to admit, guarding his heart was getting more and more difficult. The more he got to know her, the more he liked. He tried to convince himself that he was only interested in getting to know her better because she ran Tikaani. He had to get to know her and the way the business operated so he could make his father proud, right? He watched her move along the river and couldn't keep the admiration from his gaze. Denying his feelings was a losing effort. He was falling for Zoey Kirk.

Now he had to decide what, if anything, he was going to do about it.

Zoey watched as Josiah paddled away from her, giving her some space. The man could surely be infuriating! Maybe the rest of the world focused on the bottom line and high profits, but Tikaani Tours had always been about preserving nature and sharing the beauties of God's majesty—not making a buck. She would have to convince him of that as they moved forward. She'd let her emotions get the best of her during their conversation, and now she regretted her lack of tact. She'd been defensive instead of professional. She stretched, promising herself that she would handle future conversations with her new boss more diplomatically.

She glanced up and watched him navigate around a crop of rocks near the middle of the river. She was leery of Josiah's take-charge attitude as well. Was he going to come in and make drastic changes to the way she ran things, just to ensure higher profits? He didn't seem like that kind of man, yet from bits and pieces he had said during the short time she'd known him, he seemed to be out to prove something. He'd already overcome immense physical obstacles. What more did he have to prove? Was he going to destroy Tikaani and everything she loved about the company in his quest to demonstrate to the world that he was a consummate businessman? Sure, Tikaani was just a small, insignificant Alaskan tour company, but bigger wasn't always better. She'd heard that old saying "go big or go home," but in this business, that was definitely not her philosophy. Small with only three guides was just how she liked it. Chase had been satisfied as long as she made a profit each season, and he had obviously kept himself occupied with other business interests that had undoubtedly demanded more of his attention. That had always been fine with her, and she had appreciated his hands-off approach once he had given her the reins.

Was all of that about to change?

Yet even as the fear of drastic company transformation assailed her, she also had to admit that she was glad Josiah was here on this trip, offering support. She'd never even had a camper break a bone before, and now two of her charges had been murdered. It was unthinkable, yet it had happened, and on her watch. Would the company go under, as he suggested? This was a lot more serious than just a bad review on a social media page. Bankruptcy was certainly a possibility, but in her mind, the more immediate concern was just keeping the rest of the campers alive until they reached the Nuka camp. Would there be another murder? Fear was now her constant companion, and unfortunately, it only served as a grim reminder of the abuse she had suffered back in college. She thought she'd buried those memories forever, but apparently she'd never truly healed from that intense pain that had ruled her life for so many years. Now it had resurfaced and made her on edge and more suspicious than she'd like to admit.

She continued to watch Josiah carefully as he navigated the river. Although her last relationship was a dismal failure, she couldn't deny the attraction she was beginning to feel toward Josiah, even when he aggravated her. He was physically strong, despite his leg injury, but she was convinced he would never hurt her, regardless of that corporal strength. In fact, she was beginning to finally feel at ease around him. Even when his questions annoyed her, she didn't feel physically threatened. Gradually, she could feel her heart softening toward him. But did Josiah feel anything for her? It was hard for her to tell, and because it had been so long since she had even considered the possibility of a relationship with someone, she didn't trust her instincts—especially when they had led her astray so drastically in the past. Was she willing to risk dating someone again? That was really the first question she needed to answer. The mere idea filled her with trepidation, yet if she was being honest with herself, she had to admit there was a small part of her, however tiny, that yearned for that closeness again. But was Josiah the one? Could she ever open her heart to trust him?

ELEVEN

"Josiah?"

Josiah rolled over in his sleeping bag. He vaguely thought he heard someone calling him, but he was tired from lack of sleep, and he was in the middle of a very pleasant dream. Zoey was smiling at him, holding out her hand so she could take his and lead him somewhere bright and sunny. Her eyes were vibrant with life, and her lips were full and tempting.

"Josiah?"

He shook his head as the images instantly disappeared and the voice outside his tent registered. It was low but urgent, and it also belonged to the woman whom he had just been dreaming about.

"Josiah, it's me, Zoey. Are you awake?"

"Yeah, give me a sec." He sat up and rubbed his eyes as the sleep dissipated. The rain had stopped but the air was heavy with humidity and felt sticky and sweet.

"We have a problem."

The fear in her voice instantly sobered him, and he quickly reached forward and unzipped the tent flap, revealing Zoey on the other side. She was dressed in her usual camp outfit—black track pants and a red flannel shirt, but her dark brown hair hung loosely around her shoulders, and her eyes were rounded and reflected the light from the moon as she crouched by his tent. Anxiety filled her features, and his heart sped up in response.

"What's going on?"

"I'm sorry to wake you, but somebody is rummaging around by the kayaks. Can you come with me to check? I didn't feel safe going by myself." She was whispering, but he could still hear the tremor in her voice.

She was scared, and she was asking for his help.

He quickly realized that seeking his assistance must have been difficult for her. "Of course." He pulled himself up and silently put on his jacket, then exited his tent. Zoey was an extremely capable woman whose life experiences had made her fiercely independent. He knew that she wouldn't have asked for help unless she was truly afraid.

The group had made it down the river to their next campground, but the campers had all been subdued during most of the trip and had said very little. Once they'd arrived and set up camp, Josiah and Zoey had called the group together, despite the rain, and outlined new rules that everyone had to follow for the remainder of their time together. Everything had to be done in twos, and everyone would take individual two-hour shifts during the night to guard the camp. If something happened during someone's shift, they would automatically be considered the guilty party and would be handed over to law enforcement at the Nuka camp. No one was exempt.

Josiah pulled out his flashlight but didn't turn it on.

Instead, he used the light from his watch to check the time. It was almost two in the morning. He quickly glanced around the area. They had some moonlight to go by, and a few embers were still glowing in the camp-fire behind the ring of stones, sending dancing shadows against the nearby trees. The light seemed like it was enough to keep them from stumbling around in the dark, but he kept the flashlight handy, just in case. He didn't want to alert anyone to their presence as they approached the landing, and he hoped they just might be able to sneak up on the perpetrator. His heart was thumping against his chest as adrenaline and anticipation pumped through his limbs. Finally, they might discover the identity of the murderer.

"It's Nolan's turn to guard the camp. Have you seen him?" He kept his voice low, barely audible, and Zoey leaned closer to hear him, then shook her head. He could smell the outdoors in her hair, and he felt the warmth radiating from her body. Minty steam issued from her mouth as she responded.

"When I went to sleep, Lucas was on duty. I'm assuming he's back in his tent, but I have no idea where Nolan is, unless he's the one down by the kayaks."

They moved quietly around the camp and found Nolan propped up against a tree trunk, snoring. So much for having a guard. Disgust swept over Josiah and mixed with the other sentiments he was feeling. Didn't this man care that his laziness was putting everyone in danger? He crouched in front of Nolan and put his hand over the man's mouth to keep him from shouting out, then shook him on the shoulder with his other hand. Nolan came instantly awake and his eyes widened. He took in what was happening and his expression changed from fear to embarrassment as he became aware of his predicament. Josiah put his finger against his lips to silence him, then slowly removed his hand. He would chastise Nolan later. Right now, Josiah intended to enlist the man's help.

"Somebody's messing around with the kayaks," Josiah murmured softly. "Before you went to sleep on guard duty, did you see anyone up and moving around?"

Nolan rubbed his eyes and shook his head. "Nobody. I haven't seen or heard a thing."

"Small wonder," Josiah muttered as he stood again. "Follow us, and stay quiet," he ordered.

Zoey led the way down to the rocky bank where the kayaks had been stored for the evening. It was about fifty yards from where they were camping, which was unusual, but necessary in this particular campground because of the rockiness of the ground near the river.

Josiah heard something and grabbed Zoey's arm with one hand and motioned for Nolan to stop with the other. The three froze and listened. Mosquitoes were zipping around their heads, but Josiah could also hear a low scraping sound. A moment passed, then another. Zoey reached over and squeezed Josiah's hand, then released it and motioned with her head toward the noise. The three started moving forward again, silently and slowly for safety's sake, and so they didn't alert the perpetrator of their presence.

They made it another few yards and the scraping sound got louder. Then Nolan took a step and a twig broke under his weight and made a loud cracking sound. The three froze and waited, and Josiah listened carefully to see if the perpetrator had heard the noise. A beat passed. Then another. His muscles tensed, ready to react.

Suddenly, they heard a crashing sound, as if the wrongdoer realized he or she was about to be caught and had decided to run before being identified. Tree branches broke and rocks shifted as the footsteps receded, and Josiah could hear a grunt and subsequent thump as the person hit the side of a tree in their quest to avoid being seen.

Josiah didn't wait. He ran after the offender, all hope of staying silent forgotten as he flipped on his flashlight and used the beam to alternately illuminate his path and flash toward the sounds of the person escaping into the woods. The light caught the motion of a dark shape leaving the area, but as the three arrived at the kayaks, Josiah couldn't even tell if it was a man or woman who had been messing around with the boats, nor the color of their clothing, nor the shade of their hair. It was just too dark. However, there was one way to discover the identity of the perpetrator. "Let's get back to camp and see who's not in their tent. Hurry!"

Zoey's whole body felt like it was on fire as she raced back toward the campground, following Josiah and his bobbing flashlight. Fear flowed within her as she tried to hurry but also stay safe as she navigated the woods. She heard a crash behind her, and Nolan cried out as he hit the ground, hard. She slowed, caught her breath on a gasp and returned to Nolan's side. He had misjudged the height of a tree branch and caught his foot on the wood, sending him sprawling into the muck below. Pine needles and leaves now coated his clothes, as well as a liberal layer of mud. He grabbed his leg and grunted as he tried to stand.

"Are you okay?" she asked, real concern in her voice. She wanted to catch the murderer just as much as the others, but not even discovering the identity of the criminal was worth leaving an injured man in the woods.

"I will be," Nolan replied, his breath coming in huffs. "I just landed wrong on my knee. Give me a minute to shake this off."

Josiah had also returned, and between the two of them, they were able to get Nolan back on his feet. He rubbed his leg and took a few experimental steps. "I think I'm done running, but I can make it back to camp if I take it easy. You two go ahead and see if you can get back before the killer does."

Zoey met Josiah's eyes and hesitated, but Nolan spoke up again. "Go ahead. I'm fine, I promise. I can make it back if I go slowly and use the moonlight to see. Go." He motioned with his hands, in the general direction of the camp.

Zoey nodded in agreement and glanced back at Josiah once again, then returned her gaze to Nolan. "Okay, but take it easy, and if you don't make it back in a few minutes or so, we'll come back for you."

Nolan nodded and again motioned for them to leave him. "Okay. Go. I promise I'll be fine."

Josiah pointed his flashlight toward the path and

Zoey reached out and grabbed his other hand, knowing he would guide her the best he could as they headed back to the tents. They had slowed their pace but were still moving as fast as they could safely manage through the woods. A short time later, they arrived at the camp, and Josiah flashed his light around the tents. Nothing looked amiss as they stood at the perimeter. Zoey's eyes darted from tent to tent, straining her ears to hear any movement or telltale signs that someone had just returned.

"We don't have a choice," she said quietly. "We're going to have to start waking people up." Webster's tent was closest. She dropped Josiah's hand, then crouched in front of the tent flap. "John? Are you in there?" Nothing. Frustration filled her. She doubted they would find anything now since so much time had passed. Nolan's fall had given the killer the extra time he or she needed to get back to the camp and hide any evidence of their escapades. She sighed. It didn't matter. She still had to attempt to discover the identity of the murderer, even if the search yielded nothing but the anger of everyone they woke up.

She flicked the fabric on the tent and tried again. "John Webster, are you awake?"

This time, her words were met with a rustling sound. She looked up and saw that Josiah had moved to the next tent and was confronting Rick. A moment later, she returned her attention to Webster, who had just stuck his head out the tent flap. His graying hair was in disarray, and his face was puffy from sleep. "What's going on?" he asked. "Is there a problem?" He seemed rather out of breath, which didn't seem to match his appearance. Zoey wasn't sure what to think.

"No, just go back to sleep," Zoey responded softly. "We heard some noises out by the kayaks and wanted to make sure everyone was okay."

"I've been in my tent the whole time, I promise," he said, his voice rough and a tad bit defensive. "I was asleep until just now."

"No worries. Go back to bed. We'll talk more in the morning." She stood and went to stand by Josiah, who had just finished checking on Rick and his wife.

"It wasn't them," he said softly, before she had a chance to ask. "Let's check Lucas and Mia."

She nodded and followed him to their tent. They both crouched by the door, and Zoey called out to the occupants. "Lucas? Mia? Are you in there?"

Again, she heard some rustling, but eventually, Mia opened the flap enough for Zoey to see her face. Josiah had stayed with her for this tent check, apparently also wanting to hear their alibis, if they had one. "What? Do you need something?" Her hair was also mussed, yet Zoey noticed she was still wearing her makeup. She wondered absently if the woman had permanent makeup, or if she just never removed it.

"We heard someone out by the kayaks," Zoey explained again. "Were either of you just out there by the river?"

"Not us," Mia responded with a yawn. "You woke us up."

"Is Lucas in there?" Josiah asked.

Mia shifted her glance from Zoey to Josiah and narrowed her eyes. "Of course. He's in here sleeping.

Where else would he be? Are you accusing him of something?"

"No, Mia," Zoey assured her quickly. "We're just checking to make sure everyone is accounted for and safe."

Mia shrugged and pulled back the tent flap a bit more so Zoey could see inside the tent. Lucas was inside his sleeping bag and glared at them as Josiah shone his flashlight in and the beam caught his face. Was he flushed like he had just been exerting himself? It sure seemed like it, but Zoey wasn't sure enough to voice her concerns out loud. The man did glare at her, but that could be because she had just woken him up. "Has Lucas been with you all night?"

"Yes, he sure has," Mia confirmed. "Now if you don't mind, I'd like to get back to sleep before we have to get up and get back on the river. I'm a little sore from all of that exercise and need my rest."

"Of course," Zoey said. She stood and backed away from the tent as Mia abruptly zipped it closed. Zoey turned to Josiah and motioned toward the next tent. They checked each one, but everyone was in the camp and accounted for, except for Nolan, who was obviously innocent. Frustration filled her. They were no closer to learning the identity of the perpetrator than they had been before this whole episode began.

Zoey put her hands on her hips as the thoughts swirled in her brain. Lucas seemed guilty, but what if she was wrong? She'd already admonished the other campers from engaging in rampant speculation several times during this trip. She didn't want to go down that same trail.

She turned to Josiah. "I guess we'd better go check on Nolan."

Josiah nodded but put out his hand again, ready to help guide her in the darkness. She reached out and took it, grateful for the assistance. It was warm and strong in her grasp and gave her a measure of comfort as they turned back toward the trail they had just come from. His limp was quite noticeable, and she felt him tense with every step. She worried he had overdone it in their race back to camp, but she knew intuitively it would be a mistake to ask him about it. She grimaced. Although she was concerned about Josiah's injury, that wasn't her primary worry. Inside, she was terrified.

Because once again, the murderer had eluded them.

TWELVE

"It has to be Lucas," Josiah said softly, keeping his voice down so only Zoey could hear him. They had gotten Nolan back to camp and were now several yards away from the tents, talking through everything that had happened while also keeping a careful eye on the campground. "Did you see the way he looked in that tent? It sure didn't seem like he had been sleeping, and Mia looked like she had been up as well."

"I agree, but what about John Webster? He was breathing hard when I checked on him."

"But Lucas looked alert and sweaty, like he had been running and had just gotten back to camp."

"Yet if that's true, Mia just covered for him. Why would she do that if he was really guilty?"

A muscle twitched in Josiah's jaw. "Maybe she doesn't want her husband jailed? He's the primary breadwinner for that family, according to something Patricia told me the other day." He rubbed the stubble on his jaw. "Lucas was leading the charge against Webster, probably to throw the guilt off his own shoulders, and he was the one trying to burn my tent."

"And Mia was the one who looked like she was drowning me, so maybe they are working together. Or maybe the group was right all along and Webster killed Marty Garcia." She twisted her hands together. "Good grief! I just don't know. I hate to speculate, but it's obvious that the perpetrator isn't finished and we're all still in danger." Her hands moved to her arms and she rubbed them up and down, hugging herself.

Josiah tried to think of anything else besides pulling her into his arms and comforting her. Would she even allow the embrace? He wasn't sure. He patted his pocket. "I sure wish one of us knew shorthand. Then maybe we could gain some insight from Patricia's notebook." He nodded toward Zoey's waistline, where she had clipped the handheld radio. "Any news from the base camp?"

"I just reported what happened via text, but really, all we know is that someone was messing around with the kayaks. We'll have to examine everything once the sun is up to make sure nothing was sabotaged. The base camp assured me they would have law enforcement waiting for us at the Nuka camp, but that's still another day and a half away. Do you think we can make it there without anyone else getting hurt?"

"I sure hope so," Josiah said softly. Even in the shadows, he could see the worry lines across her forehead as she frowned. "A lot will depend upon what we find when we check out the kayaks in the daylight. I hope the guilty party didn't do too much damage." He took a step toward her, wincing as he put too much weight on his leg, and she reacted instantly. She took his arm and encouraged him to lean heavily on her as she led him to a nearby outcropping of white granite. He appreciated the assistance and was both surprised and delighted when the two of them ended up sitting side by side on the rocks. She hadn't flinched or even pulled back, despite their closeness. He watched her carefully for any sign of distress, but she seemed okay with the proximity, even after a few minutes had passed. Nolan had added wood to the campfire, which added a bit of light, even though it was pretty far away, but the moon reflected off her face and made her skin glow.

Despite the fear he saw etched in her features, he still thought she looked incredibly beautiful. She wasn't a classic beauty, like the models who walked a runway, but her attractiveness was magnified by the character and strength he also saw reflected in her face, and he found himself unable to look away. He was mesmerized by how the moonlight played across her skin and the way her hair framed her face.

He shook his head, trying to get those persistent thoughts out of his mind so he could focus on the here and now. He didn't need to be thinking about Zoey's allure. He needed to be trying to figure out who the murderer was so he could keep Zoey and the rest of the campers safe. "I'm tired, but I'm up now and don't know if I can go back to sleep or not. Too many thoughts are swimming around in my head." He rubbed his injured leg absently. "Those woods were like an obstacle course and reminded me of basic training. My leg is really letting me know I did too much."

"I wish I had some ice," Zoey said, her eyes filled with concern.

He instantly regretted his statement. The last thing he wanted her to worry about was his health. She had enough on her mind with getting this group home again. "It's not a big deal," he said softly. "The stiffness will work itself out if I rest it a bit." He changed the subject. "I wonder what my dad would do if he were here right now." He raised an eyebrow. "What do you think?"

Zoey was silent for a few moments as she watched the flames in the campfire. Finally, she turned to him. "Why?"

Josiah was surprised by her question. "Well, it was his company, and I was just wondering if I'm on the right track or not. You seemed to know him pretty well, so I was hoping you'd share your thoughts. Although he never had a similar situation, I'm sure he faced difficulties that tested his leadership abilities."

"True," Zoey said. "We could sit here and speculate. But the bottom line is that he's not here any longer, and now it's your company. So, the real question isn't what he would have done, but what do you want to do?"

Josiah considered her words. "I guess I just don't want to damage his legacy by making the wrong move. The murders already might spell the end for Tikaani Tours, like we talked about before, and I might not be able to salvage it. Everything depends upon what happens in the press after we get back to the base camp and what law enforcement discovers. Everyone who's scheduled to join us for the rest of the summer might suddenly call and cancel their reservations as soon as word gets out that two people actually died during the expedition. But no matter what happens, it's important to me that I keep my father's companies strong and profitable, so I need to do whatever it takes to make that happen. That's what he would have wanted. It would help me if I could figure out what he would have done in a similar situation."

"Do you have doubts about your own abilities?"

Without knowing it, she'd just hit the nail on the head. Could he even admit his insecurities here, in the deep woods in Alaska, to a woman he'd only known a few days? On some level, the whole idea seemed absurd. Yet Zoey was easy to talk to and had overcome a difficult past. She was obviously a very strong and capable person. She'd also known and worked with his father, and Chase Quinn had valued her opinion. "I'm not a businessman. I'm so new to all of this management and financial work. It's very different from commanding a company of soldiers. Yet here I am, trying to make a go of it without much experience. I have a lot to learn." He nudged her playfully. "Even you told me I was wrong when I asked about increasing Tikaani's profits."

"I sure did," she agreed. "But no matter what I say, or what Chase did in the past, the bottom line is that you have to decide what works for Josiah Quinn. Just because something worked for your father doesn't mean it will necessarily work for you, and vice versa. You're going to have to find your own rhythm and stride in this new role. And there's nothing wrong with that. In fact, it's an excellent opportunity to define your beliefs and what you stand for. These are your companies now.

From here on out, they're going to be a reflection of you, not your father."

He considered her words. "You're right, but while I'm finding my way, I don't want to make any mistakes and destroy what he created."

"There's little chance of that," Zoey said with a smile. "I have a feeling you will be successful with anything you attempt. But making mistakes and recovering from them is part of the process. It's okay to fail sometimes. It makes you a better person." She winked at him. "Look at what you've done so far, Josiah. You've walked when they told you you couldn't. Just remember, with God, all things are possible."

He tilted his head and gave her his own smile in return. "That's very true." He reached over, very slowly and deliberately, and took her hand in his own. "So, you're a Christian?"

Even though he'd given her a chance to avoid his touch, she didn't pull her hand away, and once again, he was delighted that she allowed the contact. He rubbed his thumb gently over the back of her hand. How did a trail guide end up with such soft hands? It was an enigma.

"I am," she acknowledged. "My faith is very important to me, although I have to admit, I've let my relationship with God suffer ever since I came to Alaska. This trip has been a great reminder, though, about what is actually important in life." She sighed. "I don't know why I've been hesitant to return to church. I guess it's just been easier to stay away from people, and unless I'm leading a tour, I tend to keep to myself."

"What about when you teach? The community college must be filled with new people each semester."

"To some degree, I guess you're right, but I try to keep my classes small, and for some reason, in my mind, it's different when the students are all so much younger than me and everyone is online. The computer is like a buffer, and I don't really have to get close to anyone."

He didn't challenge her on that supposition but instead asked another question. "So why do you want to stay away from others and be by yourself in the first place?" He'd just divulged his fears. Would she be willing to do the same? He found himself almost holding his breath, hoping she would feel comfortable enough to share her thoughts with him.

Zoey shrugged but still didn't pull her hand away. "I know it doesn't make much sense, especially since both of my jobs are better suited to extroverts." She ran her tongue over her teeth, a motion that he'd discovered she did regularly when she was thinking. He liked that he was coming to know her mannerisms and body language. He wanted to get to know her better. He tried to tell himself that it was friendship he wanted and needed from Zoey—especially if they were going to continue working together. But he knew he was fooling himself. He did want friendship. But did he want more as well?

Her words broke into his thoughts. "I guess, if I'm being honest, I'd have to say that I'm hiding in plain sight here in Alaska. I'm afraid to get too close to anyone, so having tour groups and classes of new people each semester makes it easy for me to avoid any long-term relationships. People come and people go. Even with God, I've struggled with the idea of Him still loving me with all of my history and problems. I think I've been afraid to pursue that relationship as well because I can't hide my faults from Him. He knows me and all of my insecurities." She turned and caught his eye. "Do you know what verse amazes me more than any other in the whole Bible? It's the one that says God thinks about each of us more than the number of grains of sand on the beach. Or something like that. I mean, isn't that just astounding to you? He knows the number of hairs we have on our head. He thinks about me and loves me even when I don't deserve it. That whole idea is really hard for me to comprehend sometimes. It just seems too good to be true."

"That is hard to fathom." Josiah shifted, moving closer to her so he could get a better look at her eyes in the dim moonlight. "You're not blaming yourself for how your boyfriend treated you, are you?"

Zoey sighed. How could she explain how she had survived over the past eight years? Sometimes, it was hard to even put her thoughts into words. "I did blame myself for a really long time. I didn't understand how somebody that said they loved me could be so cruel. But his behavior went way beyond just physical abuse. He wanted to control me—everything I did and said, and even my thoughts. At first, I just thought he was being attentive, and I was so flattered by his attention. But then I felt smothered. I thought I must have done something horrible to cause his love to turn into such a noose around my neck." She grimaced. "Well, you saw for yourself only yesterday. I still cringe if someone gets too close." She bit her bottom lip. "I'm still working on that," she admitted, chagrined.

He gave her a reassuring smile that instantly helped quell the uneasiness that had started to tie a knot in her stomach. She loved the way his smile lit up his entire face. She didn't like talking about her past, but she also realized that she needed to sort out and manage these emotions rather than hiding them away, deep inside her. If she didn't deal with them, then her old boyfriend would still be controlling her, even from thousands of miles away in his prison cell. She couldn't let that happen.

She looked at their joined hands and realized she liked Josiah's touch, and for the first time in years, she didn't feel threatened by a man sitting so close to her. It was an odd, and yet very satisfying, realization. He was actually a very attractive guy and would only grow more so as he aged. His dark brown eyes were clear and direct, and his face showed compassion, intelligence and a confidence she admired. His short brown hair accented his high cheekbones and wide brow, and his facial stubble gave him an air of mystery and appeal. She felt a warmth spread through her, and she gave his hand a gentle squeeze. Despite the stress and horrific deaths they had seen on this trip, she found herself leaning more and more on Josiah's strength, rather than hiding and pulling away. Brick by brick, he was slowly tearing down the wall that surrounded her heart. She even liked sharing her thoughts and fears and having someone to talk to who wasn't going to judge her and point out her faults.

But that was what scared her.

THIRTEEN

"I don't see any damage to any of the kayaks except a little scraping on one of the rudders that didn't cause any real damage," Zoey noted as she stood and brushed the dirt off her pants. She had looked at the skegs, rudders and bottoms of the boats, and also inspected all of the paddles. "I have no idea why someone was out here messing with them, but it looks like no harm was done."

Josiah also righted a blue kayak and stood. "I don't see anything wrong with this one either. I think that's the last of them. We checked them all." He put his hands on his hips. "Hopefully, we interrupted the intruder last night before they were able to really sabotage any of them."

Zoey walked over to the riverbank and eyed the water, then motioned to Josiah. "I guess we can head back to the camp. Are you ready?" She was eager to get back on the river and continue on their trek, but a safety check had been her first priority. In her mind, the sooner they got to the Nuka campground, the better. As it stood, they would have one more night camping, and then the group should reach Nuka around eleven in the morning the next day.

Josiah nodded and the two returned to where the rest of the group was busy packing up their tents and other supplies. Their breakfast of granola with cranberries and brown sugar was done, and all the dishes were washed and stored as well. On most trips, the group would have been laughing and enjoying the break in the rain, but the campers who met Zoey and Josiah when they returned were somber and silent, staring at one another with suspicion and trepidation. She felt the coldness from them, and the heavy feeling made her shiver involuntarily. She called the group together so she could go over some of the day's challenges before they launched.

"Although the rain has passed, the weather has left us another gift. The river is high and running really fast today. Because of everything that's happened, though, it's really important that we keep going."

"Are you saying it isn't safe to kayak today?" Nolan asked.

"No, I'm not saying that at all. What I am saying is we need to be more vigilant than normal, and I need all of you to follow instructions very carefully. This part of the river has a couple of hydraulics, or holes, where the water rushes over some rocks and then flows backward a bit to fill in the low pressure from where the water is moving faster over the rock." She motioned with her hands as she described the outcrops. "For both of them, I need you to stay on the right side of the river and avoid the rocks as best you can. Paddle by them single file and yell out if you get into any trouble at all."

"Are hydraulics dangerous?" Janey asked.

"Most are friendly and a lot of fun to go over—kind of like a fast roller coaster. Others are less friendly, and then some are just plain deadly. In this case, I'd rather just err on the side of caution due to the rain and stay away from both of them. We're all a bit stressed due to the deaths, and I think we should aim for a relaxing trip rather than takings any risks."

She went over a few more safety procedures, and then they returned to the rocky shoreline and helped everyone launch their kayaks. Once the entire group was on the water, Zoey left first so she could lead the way, and Josiah brought up the rear, making sure everyone was settled without a problem.

Even though the rain had finally stopped, a gray and rolling mist had risen, and the fog made visibility limited. She had traveled this river several times and was well aware of the twists and turns, and this section they were traveling today was the only one that gave her pause. Several trees had fallen into the water at certain points, making navigation tricky in the murky weather, and the hydraulics added another level of concern. Still, she didn't want to wait a day and hope the conditions would improve. In her mind, the risks of waiting outweighed the risks of continuing, and the base camp had texted her the day's forecast via her handheld radio that suggested the sun would make an appearance later in the afternoon.

Zoey kept to herself most of the morning and spent much of the time praying and trying to focus on the good things in her life instead of the murders. Despite the violence, she had quite a lot in her life to be thankful for. She still had her job. She was slowly conquering some of her past hurts. And they were only a day and a half away from the Nuka campsite, where law enforcement would be waiting and the murderer would finally be apprehended, if they could only figure out who it was.

Most importantly, Josiah was becoming a friend, and many of her fears about him were waning. She had been so worried that he would come in and change everything, but their camaraderie was enjoyable and growing, and she had begun to look forward to the time they spent together, even if that time was used chasing down someone bent on mischief in the middle of the night. Josiah made her feel safe, despite the violence the murderer had wrought upon the trip, and she hadn't felt that way in a very long time. It was both refreshing and invigorating.

As the group continued down the river, the clouds slowly lifted, and the visibility improved. At one point, they saw a grizzly bear and her cub taking a drink by the river's edge. Zoey and a couple of others anchored their kayaks at a safe distance and watched the two for several minutes as they frolicked around, playing in the water. The bears finally meandered back into the woods, and Zoey and the campers pulled up their anchors and continued down the river. The water was so clear below them that they could watch the fish dart past them beneath their boats. She recognized sockeye salmon, Dolly Varden trout and rainbow trout, and pointed them out to the others as they swam by. Then a rainbow appeared in the sky above them and seemed to end in a large island of trees and rocks that separated the river, and she guided the group around the island, reminding the few campers who were close by her that the first hydraulic would be just past the trees where the river narrowed again.

"Did you see those bears?" Lucas asked as Webster and Josiah approached.

Josiah nodded and Webster answered, "Yeah, we saw them. I'm glad they were across the water. That mama bear was huge!"

"Yeah, I'd hate to have her angry with me," Lucas responded. He paddled and turned his boat slightly so he could see them both better, despite the current. "You two are the last ones of the group to go past the hydraulic. Zoey asked me to stay behind and make sure everyone remembered to stay to the left once the river narrows up ahead."

"Really?" Josiah responded, trying to keep the skepticism from his voice. "I thought she mentioned earlier we needed to stay to the right as we passed the hydraulic."

"That was before she noticed how much the rain had affected the river down here," Lucas said in a matter-of-fact tone. "Now she's changed her mind and asked me to make sure everyone knows what to do and how to handle the situation before they get there."

After everything that had happened over the last few days, Josiah wasn't sure he believed Lucas, and he sure didn't trust him. Yet there was no way to verify his claim since he and Webster were the last two of the group to kayak here, and Zoey was no doubt up ahead, leading the group. None of the others were even visible now. He wished he had a way to communicate with her to confirm her instructions. He would have to fix that on the next kayak tour. "After you, then," Josiah said, motioning to the river ahead. "I'll follow behind you."

Lucas shook his head. "I would, but Zoey also asked me to make sure you went with Webster, because she has concerns for his safety since the group has been so antagonistic toward him. She wants to ensure he makes it by the hydraulic without a problem. Then I'm supposed to come behind both of you." He shrugged. "Those were her instructions."

Josiah felt a knot tighten in his gut but didn't have any reason to distrust Lucas besides his own intuition and his overall suspicion about the man. It was entirely possible that Lucas was telling the truth. But what if he wasn't? He glanced over at Webster. "What do you think?"

The other man shrugged. "What he's saying makes sense. I think if Zoey saw that the conditions had changed and needed to alter the plan, she would have left someone behind to make sure we all knew how to manage the river. I'm just surprised she chose him."

It still didn't feel right, and the knot tightened further, but without proof to the contrary, he had no remaining argument. He followed Webster's lead and paddled to the left. The river narrowed considerably, and several outcroppings of rocks separated the edge of the water from the forest beyond. There wasn't any snow left on the ground along this area of the river, but pockets of ice were still visible around some of the smaller boulders. If Zoey hadn't warned them of the danger, Josiah would have found the location both beautiful and bucolic.

The water speed increased again even more, and Josiah let the current take him around the rocks and used his paddle only to guide himself. He chanced a glance behind him to make sure Lucas was following him and was only slightly surprised to see that he was still some distance back, almost sixty yards or so, still anchored.

A cold chill swept down Josiah's spine. Had they been duped? It sure seemed like it, and Lucas had already tried to harm Josiah once. Why wouldn't he try a second time if he thought he could get away with it? It was also no secret that there was no love lost between Lucas and Webster. If Lucas had been telling the truth and they were really supposed to change sides, why wasn't he right behind them? He tightened his jaw with indecision, then sat up straighter, mentally preparing for whatever trap Lucas had set and the unknown danger that might be heading their way.

"Webster," Josiah called out. The man was about forty feet ahead of him, but he figured his voice was loud enough to carry. "Lucas isn't following us. Keep your eyes open. He might have misdirected us."

"Got it," Webster replied, not turning to look at him. "This water is running pretty fast, and it sounds like there might be a waterfall somewhere nearby. Do you hear that splashing?"

Josiah focused on the surrounding noises for a moment. There was definitely a sound of rushing water that was getting louder and louder as they approached. He looked around him pensively, but there was no way to safely navigate the rocks and return to the right side of the river.

The noise increased. It sounded like thunder, rolling and angry.

Suddenly, Webster's kayak dropped and disappeared from sight. Had he gone over a small waterfall? That was what it seemed like, but he wasn't sure. Zoey had assured him some time ago that there were no serious whitewater sections on this river. However, she had mentioned the hydraulics and a few other river hazards that any guide would have to work around to keep everyone safe. He backpaddled, trying to slow his kayak and control the bow. He quickly glanced up and to the left, and saw Webster's kayak bobbing along without him, overturned. Somehow, he had gone over a rough patch of water and was no longer in his boat. Josiah heard shouting but couldn't quite make out the words. Fear swept over him. They already knew Webster wasn't a strong swimmer. Everyone was wearing a life jacket, but even so, the shouting made it clear that Webster was in peril.

The water pushed and pulled on Josiah's kayak, making it hard to control. Suddenly, it felt as if the bottom had dropped out below him. He went over a small waterfall, only about four or five feet from top to bottom, but as his bow dropped, the water pushed his keel to the side, and his kayak dropped over the fall at a haphazard angle. Water gushed over him as the vessel turned under the weight of the water, not once, but over and over again, soaking him completely and filling his nostrils. He struggled to breathe, reaching out for anything that would pull him out of the cycle. Was this what it was like to be in a washing machine? It was an inane thought, but it still flitted through his mind as he writhed in the hydraulic.

Pain began to radiate through his chest as he struggled even more to breathe, and a tightness pulled against his lungs. He fought against the motion but had nowhere to push against to use as leverage to get himself out. He lost his paddle in the attempt to free himself and reached out desperately, trying to grasp anything that would pull him out of this nightmare. For a moment he seemed free, and he was able to suck in one small gasp of air before his kayak was ripped back into the hydraulic and once again he was tossed mercilessly in a rotating motion.

He was going to die. Today. Right here. Right now.

He couldn't breathe. Blackness threatened to engulf him as he coughed and sputtered, sure that each small gasp of air would be his last.

FOURTEEN

Zoey was terrified.

Her hands wouldn't stop shaking, and her heart felt like it was pounding so hard, it was going to burst through her chest at any moment. She had seen what happened to Webster, and no sooner had she paddled over to make sure he was safely wading to the shore than she had seen Josiah's kayak sweep over the small waterfall and get stuck in the hydraulic. Why had they gone down the wrong side of the river? She paddled quickly to the edge of the water herself, abandoned her kayak and climbed up the rock above, trying to keep Josiah's flailing body and boat in sight.

She gritted her teeth as adrenaline made her stomach twist, and for a moment or two, her muscles refused to react as she watched, frozen in helpless frustration. Then she forced herself into action and pulled the fast rope from the bag she wore on her hip. The timing of her throw had to be perfect. She waited a moment or two, then pitched the rope toward Josiah with all her might. She had tied a loop in the end, hoping that the lasso would catch him or give him something to hold on to as he struggled to pull himself out of the circular motion. The weight made the line uncoil as it flew in Josiah's direction. It landed near him, within a foot or two, and she desperately hoped he was able to reach out and grasp it.

Dear God, please let him grab that rope!

She knew he was probably getting disoriented from the motion of the boat and the total onslaught of the water. Terror swamped her as she watched helplessly from the edge. She yelled out, just in case he was able to hear and understand her words.

"Josiah, grab the rope!"

Other campers had paddled back and were watching in morbid fascination as Josiah struggled for his life, but none knew how to help, and Zoey ignored them all as she waited to see if Josiah could latch on. There was no telltale tug, no sign at all that he had seized the cable. She quickly pulled the rope back, coiled it again in a swift, no-nonsense motion and then prepared to try again. Her next toss got the rope even closer to him, and the cord might have even hit him near the chest in his watery deluge.

"Grab the rope!" she yelled again, still unsure if he could even hear her. She took a few steps to her right, trying to get a better view of where the rope had landed. The water was churning, making visibility difficult.

Abruptly, she felt a tug on the line. Had he been able to grab it? Hope surged within her and replaced the desperation that had been there only moments before. She rapidly found the other end of the line and twisted it several times around a nearby sapling, tied it, then dug into the ground with her legs and started pulling against the line with all of her strength.

"Pull, Josiah!" she called, still not sure if he could even hear her. "Pull yourself out!" She shortened the rope by a foot or so, repositioned her hands and strained again. Then she repeated the process and gained another foot, hope filling her.

Dear God, please save Josiah.

Inch by inch, she felt him slowly getting pulled out of the hydraulic. Thankfully, he was still in his kayak, and the bow suddenly popped forward as if it had been shot out of a gun. Then the stern quickly appeared, and he was finally free from the churning water.

Josiah's head fell forward as he struggled for breath, and he choked and sputtered as water he had swallowed streamed from his mouth and nose. His entire body shuddered as the tension finally began to ease from his shoulders and arms. He was safe! He propped himself up with his hands on the sides of the kayak, trying to gather his strength while still grasping the rope. It took him a few minutes, but he finally sat up fully again and looked around him, noticing for the first time that Zoey had been gently pulling on the rope and easing his kayak toward the shore. When he saw Zoey standing by the side of the river, he felt his heart quickly constrict. Was that love in her eyes? He might be misreading her, but there was definitely concern and relief written across her face.

She had just saved his life.

If he'd been in that hydraulic even a few seconds

more, he was convinced he would have drowned. He cleared his throat and pulled against the line, straightening his boat. He still didn't see his paddle, but he did see several of the other campers downstream out of the corner of his eye, and he was sure that one of them had probably grabbed it for him. Right now, the location of his paddle was the least of his worries.

For now, all he could see was Zoey. She gave him a tender smile as she tugged against the cable, bringing him closer and closer until he was finally near the rocky shore. She splashed into the water as he approached and met him before the bottom of the boat even touched the sand. She dropped the rope, grabbed the bow and pulled the kayak the last few feet until it was safely ensconced on the shore.

"Thank God you're alive! I was so scared! I thought I'd lost you!" She dropped beside him and put her arms around him before he could even pull himself free of the kayak, apparently unconcerned who could see them. For several minutes, he enjoyed the warmth and comfort of her arms. "I'm so glad you're safe!" She cupped his face in her hands. "Are you okay? Can you get out of the kayak by yourself, or do you need help?"

He unexpectedly felt very tired but enjoyed her fussing over him. He hadn't had someone worry about him like this in some time. "I'm okay," he responded roughly as he coughed on some water. "I think I can get myself out of the boat if my bad leg doesn't give out on me. I'm suddenly exhausted!"

"Yeah, that's what happens when you try to drink the river one gulp at a time."

Her voice was gruff, but he could still see the worry and caring in her eyes. He laughed as she verified the craft was solidly on the ground, then reached for him and helped him pull himself from the kayak. "That wasn't my intention, I assure you." He managed to stand, but just barely. Zoey grabbed his arm and pulled it over her head, then wedged herself under his arm.

"Here, lean on me," she said softly. "I'll help you." She led him carefully over to a nearby log. Pain shot up and down his bad leg, making it hard for him to put any weight on it, but with her help, he was able to make it, and he sat down heavily on the wood.

Once he was seated, she lit into him. "What were you doing on the left side of the river? I distinctly told everyone to stay to the right. I can't believe you didn't follow my directions. This isn't my first rodeo, you know. I was very specific about what you were supposed to do!" She took a breath as she paced back and forth, but she wasn't finished yet. "And you're an officer in the military? I thought you guys were trained to take orders. Have you completely lost your mind? You and Webster could both be dead right now!"

Her voice sounded both scared and furious to his ears, and he let the torrent flow without interruption. Once she stopped and fisted her hands, he reached over, took her left hand and squeezed it gently and intertwined their fingers. "I'm sorry. I should have stuck with your instructions. Lucas stayed behind and met up with Webster and me where the river started to narrow. He told us you had inspected the river and changed your mind based on the changing river conditions, and we were now supposed to go down the other side."

She shook her head, apparently flabbergasted at his words. "That lying man," she said vehemently. "I can't believe he did that." She suddenly pulled her hand free and started pacing, as if she was filled with so much restless energy that she just couldn't stand still.

"I promise it's true. Webster and I took a chance. We were unsure at first, but he seemed sincere and believable. A few minutes before we reached the hydraulic, I realized he hadn't come up behind us and that he must have lied, but by then, I couldn't get over to the right." He swallowed and coughed again, then continued once he caught his breath. "Lucas has to be the killer. He saw an opportunity and tried one more time to take both me and Webster out." He rubbed his bad leg. "There just doesn't seem to be any other explanation."

"I believe you," she soothed. "I'm just shocked. I guess a part of me was hoping the murders had stopped, despite the evidence we keep discovering to the contrary." She shook her head. "I was being foolish, I know." She breathed out heavily. "At least now we know for sure who the murderer is. But why would he be trying to hurt you? I still don't understand his motive."

Josiah shrugged. "I can't figure that out either. I've never met him before this trip and have no idea what he has against me."

She returned to his side and sat down next to him on the log again. Her shoulders slumped. "So, what now? How do we keep him from hurting anybody else?"

Josiah turned to Zoey. Today could have been his last day on earth. For the time being, he sure didn't want to spend it thinking about Lucas. At least not right now.

He was suddenly filled with emptiness. What if he had died today? What if he'd never had another chance to tell Zoey how he was beginning to feel about her? Josiah had learned a few things during his time in the military, and the most important was that tomorrow was a promise to no one. He didn't want to live with regrets. If he had died in that hydraulic, all of his growing emotions would have died with him. That would be a mistake. He slowly reached over, giving her time to realize his intent, and then gently touched her cheek with the pads of his fingers. Electricity crackled through the air. He slowly drew his fingers down to her lips and then outlined them, mesmerized. They were so soft. Their eyes locked. He was delighted that she hadn't pulled away. He leaned forward, saw her lips part, expectant—

"Hey! Are you okay, Josiah? I was worried you weren't going to pull out of that hydraulic. I thought you were dead!" Webster approached quickly, his words instantly dispelling the feeling of intimacy that had been thick in the air only a moment before.

Josiah turned, just as Zoey stood and put space between them. He dropped his hand, disappointed. "Yeah, I'll survive. You okay?"

"I'm fine," Webster replied, apparently unaware of what he had just interrupted. "But I didn't just ride a hydraulic like I was in a washing machine."

He sat on the log in the space Zoey had just vacated. "So, do you believe me now? It was Lucas all along. I never hurt Garcia."

Josiah keenly felt Zoey's absence, but Webster's words brought him back to the current problem, and he knew he had to focus on the murders and how they proceeded from here.

"I think it's time you tell me what's really been going on at Western," he said firmly to Webster, his tone scratchy as he coughed on a bit more water. "I think you know more than you've let on."

Webster raised an eyebrow. He seemed surprised by Josiah's insight and pursed his lips together, apparently considering exactly how much he should say.

Josiah stood carefully and took a step toward Webster, knowing his size and authoritative stature would help convince the man to talk. "Now would be a good time." His voice left no room for argument. "He almost killed us both."

Webster's face paled and he leaned back on the log.

Josiah leaned over him. "Webster, you work in the purchasing department of Western. Others have said you are the backbone of the company. You know everything that happened there, don't you? It's time to end your silence—no matter the consequences."

FIFTEEN

Webster sighed. "I wanted to tell you what was going on, but by talking, I also incriminate myself. I knew what they were doing, and yet I did nothing to stop them."

Zoey came to stand by Josiah's side. "Maybe you should start at the beginning."

Webster turned away for a moment and looked at the ground, and then looked up at Josiah. "Western is about to go into bankruptcy. Garcia had been committing fraud and embezzlement, and has brought the company down to its knees. If you check the accounts, you'll see that he had created several suppliers that didn't actually exist. He paid them with Western funds, and then the money ended up in his personal account in the Cayman Islands. I traced it there, but he found me scanning the incorporation papers, and after that, he put my name on some of them, so then I was implicated as well. He forged my signature, so now it looks as if the two of us conspired together to create the entire scheme." He pursed his lips. "I could never reveal his crimes, because he did a pretty good job of making me look guilty as well, and I sure didn't want to go to prison for a crime I didn't commit."

"So you never reported any of this?"

"To my shame, I did not. I feel horrible about it now. If I had told the board, maybe they could have stopped Garcia before the whole company was destroyed. He was just such a convincing liar. I was afraid, and I let that fear make the decision for me. I'm so sorry."

"What about Lucas Phillips?" Josiah asked. "What role did he play?"

"Lucas also found out about the embezzlement, but while I went along with it to stay out of trouble, Lucas refused. In fact, he wanted to save Western, but he didn't find out about the financial problems Garcia caused until a few months ago. He tried to save the company and even put some of his own money in to try to cover up the deficits, but by that time, it was too late. The damage was just too deep. When he realized Western was still headed for bankruptcy, Lucas confronted Garcia, and they fought about the embezzlement right before the trip and must have fought again when he murdered Garcia in his cabin. I'm pretty sure that Lucas had planned to turn us all in to the authorities as soon as this trip was over, but then he killed Garcia, so he couldn't go to the authorities after all without admitting his own guilt."

"What about Patricia?" Josiah asked. "How did she fit into the mix?"

"That I don't know," Webster responded. "All I can do is guess. From the things I've heard her say during this trip, she must have known about the embezzlement, even if she didn't know who the true culprit was. She was a terrible gossip, though, and I imagine that she was killed to keep her quiet before she found out the truth."

"That explains why Lucas wanted to hurt the others, and why he wanted to hurt you," Zoey said. "But what about Josiah? Josiah was never involved with Western. What possible reason could he have for trying to kill him?"

"It was your father," Webster revealed, looking Josiah in the eye. "He discovered Garcia's embezzlement as well, but instead of doing something about it, he sold his shares in the company and abandoned us all to deal with the mess. He took his money and left Western without reporting anything to the board or the authorities."

"And how is that my fault?" Josiah replied.

"You are the heir of all of Chase's other business enterprises. You benefited by his actions. When your father pulled out, he took a large part of the money with him. Lucas needed that money to keep the business afloat while he tried to repair the damage Garcia had caused. Your father saved himself and abandoned everybody else that worked for or had a stake in Western's success. Lucas was angry and never could forgive Chase for his selfishness. Now Western is weeks away from bankruptcy, but there's absolutely nothing we can do to stave it off, despite Lucas's efforts. The company will fold, the embezzlement will be brought to light, and Lucas and I will both go to prison. It's inevitable now." He shrugged in a defeated gesture. "I doubt Lucas actually planned on killing Garcia when he went to confront him in his cabin, but as you can tell, Lucas has a hot temper, and I'll say this for him—he really cared about Western. He put his heart and soul into that company, and now, despite all of his efforts, he's going to prison."

Josiah felt a large knot form in his throat. He'd thought his father was a business guru who never failed, and yet Webster spoke with such earnestness that Josiah could feel the truth of his words. His father wasn't such a genius after all. In fact, he'd been selfish and mercenary in his actions. How could his father have acted with so little integrity? How could he have benefited when an entire staff of people were about to have their lives ruined? Chase Quinn should have rolled up his sleeves and worked to save Western, but instead, he had taken his money and run. It was a bitter pill to swallow.

Josiah felt nauseated. Little balls of sweat popped out across his forehead, and he felt himself sway slightly on his feet.

Zoey noticed immediately. "You should sit," she said softly as she led him back to the log where he had been sitting only moments before.

He lowered himself down as thoughts swirled in his head. He'd never seen the greedy, self-absorbed side of his father that Webster had just described, but knowing his father how he did, he didn't doubt that it existed. In fact, maybe he had been willfully blind to his father's faults and subconsciously chosen not to see the unsavory behavior. Images from past discussions filled his head, and he filtered through them, trying to differentiate between the man he knew and the man who was being revealed.

Zoey turned to Webster. "You still haven't answered my question. Why would Lucas take out his anger on Josiah? Josiah had nothing to do with the problems at Western. Being the heir in this day and age is a ludicrous reason to try to take a man's life."

Webster shook his head. "When a man is desperate and angry, he doesn't need much more. Lucas can't hurt Chase any longer, but he can still get his revenge on Chase's son. That's a pretty powerful motive."

Josiah coughed, again sputtering up water that was still in his system from his battle with the hydraulic. Zoey tried to help him, but there was nothing she could really do. He swallowed, coughed again and finally regained his breath after a moment or two. He couldn't seem to keep images of his father from filling his mind. But now, instead of pleasant memories, the negative ones began to surface. His father punishing him severely for getting his first B in school. His father throwing a tantrum when Josiah didn't make first string his freshman year on the football team. His father berating him when he had failed to keep the relationship strong with his scheming girlfriend. Chase Quinn hadn't been as perfect as Josiah had pretended. Maybe he didn't want to emulate his father's business tactics after all.

Zoey patted Josiah's back, a feeling of helplessness assailing her as she watched Josiah not only try to recover from his episode in the river but also deal with the revelation of his father's past behavior. It was easy to love someone and ignore their faults. She was an expert at it and had loved her old boyfriend and ignored the abuse, hoping that the love she'd felt would be enough to hold their relationship together if he would only change his behavior. The situations were very different but still gave her some insight into a small part of what she thought Josiah was going through. Although he was attempting to be stoic in his response, she was slowly getting better at reading him, and now she could see pain etched in his features that hadn't been there only moments before.

"He made mistakes," Zoey said softly. "But he still loved you."

"Did he?" Josiah replied bitterly. "How could he have been so selfish and so uncaring about the needs of others?"

Before she even had a chance to answer, Rick and Janey Hall approached the group. "What's going on?" Risk asked. "We saw Josiah struggling in the river. Are you all right?"

"I will be," Josiah responded, his voice rough. "Lucas tried to kill Webster and me. He's the murderer we've been looking for. We need to secure him so he can't hurt anyone else."

As Josiah stood, Zoey turned, noticing that others from the group were approaching. "I think we need to have a group meeting before we get back on the river," she said cautiously. She wasn't sure how the campers were going to react, but for the first time since they'd started this expedition, she felt confident that they were on the right track. "Let's get everyone together down by the kayaks. Rick, can you and Janey get Josiah's kayak and put it with the others?"

The two nodded and grabbed the handles on both ends of Josiah's boat, and the group followed the riverbank until they got to where the other campers had congregated. Rick and Janey left the kayak on the rocky shore by the others, then joined the group. Lucas was standing by his wife, his features tense.

"I sure hope you're okay," Jessie Chapman said as she eyed Josiah and his disheveled state. "So, what happened?" she asked to no one in particular.

Zoey put her hands on her hips. "Josiah got caught in the hydraulic that I had warned everyone about. He almost died. But that's what you wanted, isn't it, Lucas?" She turned and glared at the man who had wreaked so much havoc during this trip. "You purposely told both Josiah and Webster to go the wrong way in hopes that they would get hurt and die."

Mia's eyes rounded. "What are you talking about?" she asked, her tone incredulous.

"It's true!" Webster declared. "He misdirected us and got just what he wanted when Josiah got stuck in the hydraulic and nearly lost his life."

"Actually, if I had gotten what I wanted, you and Josiah would both be dead right now," Lucas said with a sneer in his voice.

"How could you?" Nolan said, his lip curling in disgust.

"You're the murderer?" Mia said at the same time, her voice now filled with wrath. She dropped her arms and stepped away from him, her expression black. "It can't be true!"

"I say we give him a taste of his own medicine," Nolan declared, his hands fisted. "And what about poor Patricia? That woman never did anything to you, and you stole her life from her."

Lucas pressed his lips together, apparently suddenly realizing that he had just admitted his guilt and that the group could well turn against him and hurt him right here and now. He took a step back. "You can't prove anything."

"Maybe not," Josiah said, his tone vehement. "But what just happened is proof enough for me, and I'm not taking any more chances around you." Rick handed Josiah some rope that he'd retrieved from his backpack, and Lucas glared at Josiah as he tied his hands together.

Zoey watched the two men carefully, ready to step in if the two started brawling, even though she was sure to get hurt if she got caught between them. Even Rick had backed away from them both, probably also sensing the same barely harnessed aggression that filled the air. She could tell by Josiah's movements that he was struggling to keep his temper in control, but he finished the knot and stepped back, a fury in his eyes she had never seen before. Even so, it was clear that if a fight ensued, it would be Lucas who started it, not Josiah.

She marveled at his quiet strength. Josiah was a soldier. Granted, he was an injured man and his damaged leg held him back at times, but he still had been battle-trained and could no doubt tear Lucas limb from limb if he so desired. The man had just tried to kill him, and yet

Josiah kept his emotions in check and didn't hurt him in retaliation. This was new to her. Her old boyfriend had never had such control. She marveled at it, noting the stark differences between the two men.

She had been able to insulate herself in Alaska from the rest of the world for almost eight years. Almost all her time and attention during that period had been focused on making Tikaani a successful business. She had tried to convince herself that she didn't need or want a man in her life. She hadn't thought she needed love to be happy. She could live without it. But as she thought of going on without Josiah at the conclusion of this tour, she knew that she'd been wrong. She did want love. She did want to try again and risk her heart. All men weren't the same. And Josiah Quinn was worth it.

Her thoughts scattered as Nolan approached, holding his paddle in his hands. She had been so involved in her musings that she hadn't even noticed when he had left the group and returned with it, holding it like a baseball bat. Now he stood at the head of the campers, his expression filled with hatred and wrath. "We won't be safe as long as he is alive. If we bury him here, no one will ever even find his body. It will be our secret, and we'll all finally be safe."

SIXTEEN

"Murder is not the answer," Josiah said roughly as he put his hands on his hips. He turned and looked one by one at the faces of each member of the group, who had circled Lucas and were now glaring at him with a mixture of disgust, fear and fury. Even Lucas's wife, Mia, seemed to have abandoned him and had joined the ranks of the group seeking to hurt him. "I'm just as angry as the rest of you are. After all, he just tried to kill me in the hydraulic, and he probably would have succeeded in burning my tent down if Zoey hadn't stopped him. But revenge is not the answer. We have to let the authorities do their jobs."

"Josiah's right," Zoey agreed, stepping between Nolan and Lucas. "This is a job for law enforcement. If we stop now for the day, we'll reach the Nuka campsite by tomorrow afternoon. At that point, we can hand him over to the police and let them sort this all out." She glanced around the area, then pointed to a clearing about eighty feet downstream. "We all need a break. This isn't one of our normal campsites, but I think we should call it a day. Let's set up camp down there and make some dinner.

There's some good fishing in this river. I know everyone is in a hurry to get back to civilization, but let's relax a little and let some steam off. Those that want to can get their poles and add some trout to the dinner menu."

Josiah met her eyes and nodded. It was a good time to stop and regroup. He even recognized his own need to rest and recover after his experience in the hydraulic. He was also well aware that when people's emotions were running high mistakes could happen and even more people could get hurt. That was the last thing he wanted, especially now that they'd discovered the identity of the murderer.

He grabbed Lucas's arm and escorted him with the rest of the group down to the clearing, and while the others set up their tents and started a fire, Josiah tied Lucas to a tree, his hands firmly secured in front of him. Another rope circled his chest and was tied behind the branches, forcing him to stay sitting on the ground with his back against the trunk. He must have been uncomfortable, but he said nothing further, apparently aware that he was already on dangerous footing with the group.

Once the camp was ready, several campers tried fishing in the river. Like Zoey had predicted, they found that pike and trout were plentiful, and they added their catch to the evening meal. After dinner was eaten and everything was cleaned up, Zoey shooed the campers down toward the river. "We'll stay and keep an eye on Lucas. The rest of you go fish or walk—whatever you need to do to clear the air and relax."

Josiah stood by Zoey's side until the group dispersed,

then joined her to sit on a large rock by the campfire. He reached to the ground and pulled up a long stick, then poked at the logs in the fire with it and watched as the ash flew into the sky. "I have to admit, I was a bit worried when Nolan came up with that paddle. I wasn't sure he was going to stop."

"I agree," Zoey said softly. "For a minute there, I thought he was even capable of hurting you and me if we got in his way, and that the others were going to join him in his quest for vengeance. I've been praying all afternoon, hoping God would intervene and calm these people down. Their attitudes are just downright scary. I can understand why they're upset. I mean, I'm angry and scared, too. But I never thought I'd see someone want to combat violence with even more violence. I guess a mob mentality is a real thing after all. One person stirs them up, and then the emotions are running so high that nobody can stop and think clearly." She brushed some of her hair back from her face. "I might not have believed it if I hadn't seen it for myself, up close and personal with my own two eyes."

Josiah tilted his head. "I know you said you're a Christian, but I don't think I ever told you that I'm one, too."

She raised her eyebrows and gave him a smile. "That's good to hear."

"You said you were trying to renew your relationship with God, and I think I'm in pretty much the same spot. I haven't been a very good Christian lately."

Zoey reached over and squeezed his arm in a gesture of support, then released it. "Really? Why not?"

Josiah continued to push at the logs as he tried to gather his thoughts. It was hard to explain, but he found himself wanting to reach out to Zoey and share this side of his life. "I've been struggling with my relationship with God ever since my leg got injured. I guess I expected a miraculous healing so I could instantly return to the way my body had worked before the mortar damaged the nerve. When that didn't happen, I was disappointed, and I got frustrated. If I'm being honest, I'd have to say I was even angry with God for letting me get hurt in the first place. I felt like He owed it to me to heal me. Now I finally realize how wrong that was."

"I've put God in a box before, too," Zoey admitted. "I've expected Him to act or work out a situation in a certain way and then been upset when I didn't get the solution I expected. Sometimes, it's really hard for me to see the big picture. I know God is working, but a lot of the time, I don't understand how the pieces fit together."

"That's it exactly." He considered her words for a few minutes in silence, then drew his lips into a thin line in contemplation. "I guess that's where faith comes in." Then he smiled and nudged her playfully. "Hey, you're a pretty smart cookie."

She laughed and nudged him back. Her teasing and smile delighted him. Just a few days ago, she was afraid of him and instantly retreated if he got too close. Today, she was allowing him to sit right beside her and appeared totally at ease. She had also just reached out and touched him of her own accord. He was both charmed and thankful for the change, as well as excited about the possibilities, despite the hesitance that had been weighing on his heart. It was time to come clean and see if she was feeling the same things he was experiencing. "I haven't had such great experiences with women in the past," he said softly. "But there's something between us. Something I can't deny any longer. Something I don't want to ignore." He slowly reached over and took her hand and was pleased when she allowed the contact and maintained it. Tingles of electricity shot up his arm and he smiled. He intertwined their fingers. "I realize dating someone in the military is hard. My schedule used to vary a lot, and then when I was overseas, I was away for months at a time. Still, I have to admit that I was surprised when I discovered my last girlfriend was cheating on me. It hurt so much that I didn't think I could ever trust someone again." He turned and met her eyes and enjoyed watching the reflection of the flame dance in those blue depths. "But now that I've met you, I'm beginning to wonder if it's possible."

"Possible to fall in love?" Zoey asked breathlessly.

"Possible to trust and to love again," he responded quietly. He moved his other hand to her lips and outlined them with his finger. Her skin was so soft, silky and beautiful. He knew he had to move slowly with Zoey because of her past, but that was okay with him. Right at this moment, he felt like he could sit here for hours, just getting to know the feel and touch of her lips. "You're amazing, Zoey. Do you know that? I'm really impressed with your quick thinking and how you handled everything today. You saved my life! I would have drowned for sure if you hadn't pulled me out." He lightly touched her lips again with his fingertips. "Have I thanked you yet?"

She stared up at him with her beautiful blue eyes and shook her head, appearing mesmerized by his touch. He liked the way she felt, liked the way her skin glowed in the firelight and liked the way she was watching him. He released her hand and then placed his own on either side of her face, gently cradling her. "Well, that's a problem that should be remedied immediately." He leaned in and kissed her, softly at first, then longer when she didn't pull away. She tasted sweet, like the honey they had just eaten a few minutes ago with their dessert. When the kiss ended, he kept his hands on the sides of her cheeks for a moment, then gently caressed her face with his thumbs, drawing them over her eyebrows and around her hairline before releasing her. "Thank you for saving my life."

"Wow," Zoey said as she touched her lips lightly with her fingers, a smile in her eyes. "Remind me to save your life more often."

"Help! Janey fell into the river!"

The frantic voice came from the east, immediately dispelling the intimate mood. Zoey quickly stood and saw Nolan running toward them, flailing his arms. They were a good fifty yards from the water, and although they could hear others yelling and moving by the river, they couldn't see what had actually happened. Zoey started running toward the shoreline and heard Josiah following right behind her, his uneven gait keeping up with her own, despite his bad leg.

"What's going on?" she asked quickly as they reached Nolan, who was still motioning with his hands for them to follow him. His eyes were wide with fear and his whole body trembled. All three of them ran toward the water as Nolan explained. "Janey was trying to fish and wasn't paying much attention to what was going on around her. The next thing I knew, she had lost her footing and was sputtering in the water. I think she must have hit her head or something, because she didn't seem to be able to get herself up. The current started to drag her downstream, but Rick jumped in after her and pulled her out. I came to get you while he was trying to help her."

Adrenaline pumped through Zoey's veins as they ran, and she reviewed the first-aid steps in her mind as they approached. How much could go wrong during one trip? This was unbelievable. She wanted to scream in frustration as they approached the small group that had gathered around Janey's prone body. The woman didn't seem to be breathing, and Rick was sobbing as he shook her, trying to get her conscious again. A small pool of blood had matted her hair above her left eye. Her face was pale and her lips were turning blue.

"I don't think she's breathing," Zoey said quickly. She motioned for Rick to get back and then took his place by Janey's side and leaned over her head. She watched her chest, but there was no motion, and no breath warmed her cheek. She put her arm gently under Janey's neck, repositioned it and blew in two quick rescue breaths. Water dribbled out of her mouth and nose, but then Janey's chest rose and fell, so Zoey knew that air was getting through and the airway wasn't constricted. She blew in a few more breaths, then checked Janey's pulse. At first, she couldn't detect it and felt a moment of panic, but then she moved her fingers slightly and found it—nice and strong. A wave of relief swept over her as she moved to continue the mouth-to-mouth resuscitation, but after several more breaths, Janey suddenly started coughing and a great deal more water poured out of her nose and mouth. Zoey turned Janey's head so the liquid could run out and into the ground. Then she stood by, waiting to see if the poor woman could breathe on her own or not once the hacking stopped. It took a full minute or so, but eventually the coughing subsided and Zoey could tell that Janey was breathing on her own and was starting to recover.

Relief swamped her, and Zoey carefully examined the woman's head wound, then leaned back, making room for Rick to reach his wife and pull her into his arms. "I think she's going to be okay now. That bump on her head dazed her, and she swallowed a bit of the river, but she seems to be breathing better."

"Thank God you're still alive!" Rick cried, as tears streamed down his face. "I thought I'd lost you!"

Josiah patted Rick on the back and then held out his hand to Zoey. She took it and he pulled her to her feet.

"Be careful of her head wound," Zoey said to Rick. "It may make her disoriented for a little bit, and she'll probably have quite a headache. She'll need to go back to camp and rest once she's able to walk again." She turned her attention to Janey, whose eyes were clear, despite the ordeal she'd just endured. A large bump was already forming over her eye as the swelling increased. "Janey, how are you feeling?"

"My head hurts," she sputtered with a grimace. "And my throat is sore."

"Probably from all that river water you drank," Josiah said with a shake of his head. "I just tried to do the same thing a few hours ago. It doesn't taste very good, does it?" The group laughed. Now that they knew Janey would be okay, they started dispersing, giving Rick a chance to comfort his wife in private.

Suddenly, Zoey turned to Josiah. "We left Lucas alone. We'd better get back up there."

She saw a reflection of her own worry in Josiah's eyes as the two raced to the campground. The fire was still burning brightly, and Lucas was still tied to the tree where they had left him. But now there was something totally new in his appearance.

Lucas Phillips had a bloody wound in his hair, and his head was slumped forward over his body. Another patch of blood was pooling silently in the middle of his chest, painting his shirt a dark red. Zoey called out, but the man didn't move in response. She raced to his side, stepping over a bloody kayak anchor as she crouched down and gently raised his head. His dark, unseeing eyes stared back at her.

Lucas Phillips was dead.

SEVENTEEN

"The anchor is missing from Rick's boat," Nolan reported. "But Rick couldn't have done it. He was trying to save his wife. He's probably still down there, helping her recover and taking care of her." He raked his hands through his hair. "I've asked everyone about their whereabouts during Janey's accident, but I was so busy worrying about Janey, I don't really remember who was where. Still, someone must be lying. I mean, Lucas didn't stab himself and hit his own head with that anchor. We obviously have another murderer in our midst."

A cold chill ran down Zoey's spine. "Anyone could have done this," she acknowledged fatefully. She fisted her hands over and over. "How can this be happening? We just figured out that Lucas was the culprit, and then he becomes a victim himself. It doesn't make sense!"

Mia was sitting by the fire, hugging herself and swaying back and forth, her eyes focused on the fire. Every few minutes, a soft moan issued from her lips. She seemed almost catatonic with grief.

Zoey pulled out her handheld radio and typed another message to the home base. She was really getting tired of sending messages that only had 160 characters, but this was still the only method of communication available. She had reached her wit's end and needed clear direction from someone in law enforcement. The campers were all truly terrified now and kept voicing their concerns. Who would be the next to die, and who was the new murderer among them?

The screen blinked and then disappeared as the batteries suddenly died, and Zoey felt so frustrated she wanted to throw the radio into the river. She closed her eyes, took a deep breath and then said a quick prayer, asking for guidance and strength. Then she gritted her teeth, found her backpack and replaced the batteries. Thankfully, she always kept several batteries on hand. The screen leaped back to life, and she retyped the latest message and hit Send.

When was she actually going to be able to talk to another human being at the base camp? She glanced over at Lucas's ruined body once again as trepidation swept over her from head to toe. Three people were dead. Three! It was inconceivable. She closed her eyes and leaned against a nearby tree. Was she ever going to feel safe again?

Dear God, I can't handle this on my own. I'm giving it all to You. I thought I was in control, but it's obvious that I'm not. I'm so scared. Please help us.

She glanced over at Josiah, who was standing on the other side of the camp and speaking with Nolan. She gave him a watery smile, then wiped the tears from her eyes. Where had John Webster been when she and Rick had been helping Janey? After what he'd revealed, he certainly had a motive to silence Lucas. She glanced around, looking at the faces of the other campers. What about the others? Had Nolan sneaked back to the camp while she'd been resuscitating Janey? Nobody seemed to know. She and Josiah had interrogated everyone after Nolan had started asking questions, but they had gotten very little new information. No one had seen the murderer slip away with the anchor and kill Lucas. It felt like they were starting at square one again.

Suddenly the radio crackled in her hand and she heard a voice. "This is base camp. Come in trip one. Come in."

Joy leaped within her as she pushed the talk button and raised the radio to her mouth. "This is trip one. Can you hear me?"

"Loud and clear, expedition one."

Suddenly she wanted to sing! She wanted to dance! They finally had voice contact again with the home base! Hope surged within her. Maybe, just maybe, they were going to survive this horrible trip after all. She motioned for Josiah to follow her, and the two of them walked a short distance into the woods so they'd have some privacy. Zoey could tell that Josiah was also relieved to finally have voice contact with the home base. Zoey talked to the staff for a few minutes, and then a law enforcement officer joined the call. Giving as many details as they could remember, Zoey and Josiah then managed to go over everything that had happened over the last few days. Just to unburden herself and share the details with someone in authority helped her feel a measure of relief, and a heaviness seemed to have lifted from her shoulders. She had hope again. God was answering her prayers.

Detective Lockhart from the local police department was a man with a deep voice and a slight Native American accent. He seemed anxious to hear the specifics and broke up Zoey's monologue a time or two to ask questions as she described everything that had happened. Although she'd never met him in person, she'd heard about the officer in their small community and knew he had the reputation of being a compassionate and talented investigator. He continued to ask several questions, and finally, after she and Josiah had described all they could about the three murders and other events, he started asking her questions to verify her group's current location.

"We have your GPS coordinates from the radio," he said carefully as if he was studying a map as he was talking. "I have some good news and some bad news. Which do you want first?"

Zoey never liked that game, but she took it in stride. "Hit me with the bad stuff."

There was a pause and she could hear paper rustling. Or was it just more static? She couldn't tell. "Unfortunately, it still doesn't look like we'll be able to come in and get you. You're in an area that is so heavily wooded, we can't get any air support in there, and even if we left by motorized boat at first light, we couldn't get to you very quickly either since we're leaving from the base camp. The river between here and there has some really shallow areas that we'd struggle to pass with the bigger boats, and at this point, I think it makes sense for you to just keep your group heading downstream in your kayaks until you get to Nuka."

Zoey sighed. "And the good news?"

Detective Lockhart chuckled. "Well, if we both leave early in the morning, then we can meet up with you at Nuka tomorrow in the early afternoon, just like we'd hoped. By then, I'll be able to get a few more officers up here with me, and we can make the trip from the base camp to Nuka in the motorized larger boats in about the same amount of time it will take you to get there by kayak. We can even bring you lunch."

Zoey had already pretty much figured out the schedule, but it was nice to have it confirmed. "What should we do in the meantime? One murderer is dead, but another one of these people is a killer. We're all afraid to even go to sleep tonight."

"Have the people you trust stand guard in shifts. I don't see any other solution," Detective Lockhart replied. "On this end, I can tell you that I'll be researching the embezzlement you just described and digging into Western Office Supply to find out more about these allegations. I'll also have another officer start looking into the backgrounds of your dead campers. Let's talk again in the morning before you head out. By then, I should have a much better handle on what we're dealing with."

"And what about Lucas's body?"

"Bury him before you turn in for the night. Otherwise, you'll end up getting some visitors you don't want or need while you're trying to sleep. Bears and other animals will be attracted to the blood."

Zoey agreed, then ended the call and turned to Josiah. "What do you think?" she asked, her shoulders slumped.

"I think this roller coaster we've been riding is about to come to an end. Finally." He put his hands on Zoey's shoulders and rubbed them gently. "It would have been great if law enforcement could have swooped in here right now and saved the day, but we'll see them tomorrow, which will have to work. Nolan, Rick and I can take shifts guarding the camp tonight."

Zoey tilted her head, giving him more access to the tight muscles in her shoulders. "Do you trust them? I have to tell you, after seeing Nolan threatening Lucas with the paddle earlier, I'm scared to be around him."

"I'm not happy about it either, but I do know Rick and Nolan were with us today while we were trying to help Janey. I don't know how they could have been in two places at once, and we have to trust somebody." He finished her short shoulder rub and let his hands drop.

"Are you sure Nolan was down by the river the whole time I was helping Janey? I was so focused on what I was doing that I couldn't really pay attention to who else was standing around."

"Actually, you're right. I wasn't watching him the entire time," Josiah stated with concern in his voice. "I guess it's possible he went and killed Lucas and then came back to the river. It wouldn't have taken very long to attack him with the anchor." He rubbed the stubble on his chin. "Looks like another sleepless night."

"Well, if it wasn't Nolan, we're still missing something," Zoey said thoughtfully as she secured the radio in her jacket pocket and zipped it up. "Who else would want Lucas dead?"

"Webster is the only one I can think of," Josiah conceded. "Maybe he lied about his innocence and actually did embezzle the money with Garcia. With Garcia, Patricia and Lucas dead, he doesn't have to worry about anyone else accusing him of stealing the money, and he can probably destroy any proof that might exist as soon as he returns to Western after this trip is over. That's quite a motive."

"True, but at this point, he already knows his involvement in Western's financial problems is going to come to light somehow. I doubt the three that died are the only ones that suspected he was involved. In fact, Patricia went up and down talking about Webster's role in the store's demise to anyone who would listen." Zoey paced back and forth. "Killing Lucas doesn't change that and wouldn't get him anywhere. And now that I think about it, as long as Lucas was still alive, Webster was probably hoping to get some sort of deal to get a lesser sentence if he testified against Lucas and about everything that happened at Western. Now that possibility no longer exists."

"Who else would want Lucas dead?" Josiah asked quietly. "What's the motive?"

Zoey sighed. "I honestly have no idea. Could someone else have been involved in the embezzlement?"

"Who knows?" Josiah said. "Maybe law enforcement will uncover something as they start investigating everything on their end." He reached over and pulled her into his arms. She welcomed the comfort he offered, even though her fear seemed to be chasing all the other emotions out of her—except one, guilt. How could she have been kissing this man a few short hours ago while people were dying all around her? She had let her guard down, and now another man was dead. "I should have been watching him. I knew people were upset when they found out he was the murderer." She gulped. "I shouldn't have kissed you. I should have focused on protecting him."

Josiah rubbed her back. "Neither one of us knew he was in danger, and that kiss didn't make one bit of difference to what happened. Janey needed your help, pure and simple. It was your quick thinking and actions that saved her life."

She suddenly pulled out of his arms, the guilt overwhelming her. "I was wrong. I'm so sorry. I can't do this." She backed up one step, then another. How could she have been even considering a romance when a murderer was on the loose? What had she been thinking?

Josiah let her pull away without an argument. He didn't think she had anything to feel guilty about, but he could tell by her expression that now wasn't the time to discuss it. There was something special growing between them—he was sure of it. But there would be time later once they returned to the base camp to explore their relationship. With Zoey, he knew it was going to take time for her to trust him. But she was worth the wait. Right now, his protective feelings were surging as he tried to figure out the best way to keep her safe from the killer, whoever it was, and ensure the rest of the innocent campers made it back to the home base alive. "We still have Patricia's notebook, and even Webster wasn't sure how she fit into all of this and how much she actually knew about the financial problems at Western. I sure wish we knew how to read shorthand. There have to be some clues inside."

Zoey suddenly looked up and snapped her fingers. "You're right. But just because we can't read it, that doesn't mean we can't use it to ferret out the new murderer."

Josiah frowned. "How do you want to do that?"

Zoey's eyes brightened as she talked. "We never told anyone that we found her notebook. But tonight, we can let it slip that I've got it. Everyone knows that we've been in touch with the base camp. We can also tell everyone that as soon as we get to the Nuka camp tomorrow, law enforcement will be waiting with someone who can translate the book. Then I'll pretend to fall asleep by the fire while I'm looking through it, and the killer will try to come and get it away from me."

Josiah narrowed his eyes as anger erupted within him. "I will not allow you to use yourself as bait!"

Zoey raised her eyebrow. "Allow?"

Josiah fisted his hands. "Yeah, I know, I'm not supposed to use words like that, but good grief! I'm the boss of Tikaani now. That has to mean something." He moved his hands to his hips. "You've been in danger long enough. I don't want you hurt. I couldn't stand it if you were taken away from me, especially now that we've finally found each other."

Zoey took a step forward and grasped his hand, then

gave it a gentle squeeze. "I don't want to lose you either, but I'll be perfectly safe if you help me out," Zoey said tenderly. "You can be hiding nearby, watching and waiting to see who comes to steal the book." She brought her other hand up and lightly touched his cheek. "I know if you're there with me, I'll be safe."

Josiah appreciated that she was trying to lessen his worry, and he also recognized that once again, she had initiated the contact. Even so, the bottom line was that he didn't want her in any more danger than they were already in. No matter what her plan, in his mind, it wasn't worth the risk. "I can't lose you," he said, his voice soft. "I don't know for sure where our relationship is going, but I do know that I almost died today. It made me realize how short life really is." He covered her hand with his own. "You're important to me, Zoey. I'm falling in love with you."

She took a step closer and gave him a tender smile with a look of love and sincerity in her eyes. "I'm falling in love with you, too. But I can't let the murderer get away with it. I have to do everything I can to stop them before someone else gets hurt. Together, we can identify the murderer. I'm sure of it."

He squeezed her hand and then released it. "Okay, let's go over your plan."

They went over her idea step-by-step, then returned to the campfire where the others had just finished cooking a snack of s'mores. Despite the sweet dessert, the mood was sullen and apprehensive. They all knew they still had a murderer among them, and while Rick and Janey kept sneaking suspicious looks at John Webster,

Jessie kept glaring at Nolan. Lucas's wife, Mia, was still distraught and inconsolable due to her husband's death. She had refused all food and was still rocking herself back and forth on her perch by the fire.

As Josiah watched, Zoey grabbed a marshmallow and a stick that someone else had used and started to roast it over the fire. "I have good news, everyone. The radio is finally working, and I was able to talk to our base camp. They are aware of everything that has happened to us and will be waiting at the Nuka camp tomorrow to arrest the murderer."

Nolan shook his head. "How can they arrest the murderer when we don't even know who it is?"

"Because of this," Zoey said as she pulled the small blue book out of her inner pocket and showed it to everyone. "This is Patricia's notebook. We had quite the conversation, the policeman, Josiah and I, and after we described it to him, he felt sure that whatever is in it will help us discover the killer's identity."

"You see," Josiah added, "the notebook is written in shorthand, but the cop is bringing an expert stenographer with him to the Nuka campsite who can translate it for us immediately." He glanced over at Zoey and was bolstered by the look of confidence she sent his way. He continued, "After talking to the police, we're convinced that Lucas killed Marty because he was embezzling funds from Western, and he killed Patricia because she knew about the embezzlement and was blackmailing him. This little notebook explains it all, and whoever killed Lucas must be mentioned in this book as well. Finally, we'll have answers to our questions and know the truth." Josiah wasn't sure about the blackmail at all, or exactly what the notebook contained, but he hoped his broad statements were enough to engage the killer's curiosity.

Mia stopped her rocking. "That's ridiculous. My husband tried to save Western. He wasn't being blackmailed. He was a good man."

"Well, he did kill two people, Mia," Zoey said with compassion in her voice. "But by this time tomorrow, we'll know everything, including the identity of the person who killed Lucas." She glanced sympathetically at Mia. "I hope that thought brings you comfort—at least a little. I'm sure you're anxious to know who murdered your husband."

Josiah looked at each face around the group. They had a mixture of expressions, and he still had no idea who the killer might be. Whoever had committed the murder was also the consummate actor. "Zoey is going to keep Patricia's notebook with her for safekeeping, and Rick and Nolan, I need you both to help me with guard duty. All we have to do is survive one more day. Then tomorrow, law enforcement will meet us at Nuka, and everyone will finally be safe."

The trap was set. But was it enough to catch their killer?

EIGHTEEN

The air felt thick. Josiah watched from a few feet away as he saw the silhouette approaching. His heart was beating frantically against his chest, and his stomach twisted as he saw the figure get closer and closer to where Zoey was lying by the fire on her sleeping bag, feigning sleep, with the notebook lying carelessly on top of her chest as if she had fallen asleep looking through the pages. What if he couldn't protect her? Fear made beads of perspiration pop along his brow.

Gravel crunched. A twig snapped.

The killer paused at the noise, looked cautiously around the scene and then took another step. Mere seconds later, the murderer was standing over Zoey's prone figure, raising a knife, poised to strike. The fire danced and sent shadows into the woods, making the aggressor seem even larger and more treacherous.

"Freeze!" Josiah ordered in a forceful tone. He quickly moved from behind the tree and pointed his flashlight right at the person's face who was standing over Zoey. At the same time, Zoey sat up and scooted away from the aggressor, taking the notebook with her.

Mia Phillips yelped in surprise and tried to hide the knife she had in her hand, but it was too late. It was obvious from her stance and the way she had been holding the weapon that she'd been about to attack Zoey and steal the notebook.

"Drop the knife!" Josiah commanded.

Instead of following his orders, Mia turned the blade toward Josiah and raised it threateningly over her head. "You stay away from me. I need that notebook!"

"Not a chance. You're going to prison," Josiah said forcefully. He took a step toward her, then another. Tension sizzled in the air as he closed the distance between them, making sure he was between Mia and Zoey and there was no way Mia could get around him. "You really think you're going to overpower me, Mia? It's over. I'm not letting you hurt anyone else, and that's a promise."

"Why did you do it?" Zoey asked. "Why did you kill your husband?"

"I don't know what you're talking about."

"Oh, stop with the playacting," Josiah said, handing the flashlight to Zoey. He quickly grabbed Mia's wrist and wrenched the knife from her hand. She tried to resist and pulled against his grip, but she was no match for Josiah's strength or speed. "It's obvious we can't believe anything you say. You've been lying this entire trip." Josiah secured the knife in the waistband of his jeans. Mia started to back away from them, but Josiah quickly stepped forward and grabbed her upper arm in a viselike grip, stopping her escape. "I think you intended to kill Zoey on that very first day when you tried to drown her in the bay." Zoey shone the flashlight at the two of them while he quickly searched Mia to make sure she didn't have any other weapons. Finding none, he turned her to face her again. There was hatred, fear and anger reflected back at him in her small, narrow eyes. "The question is, why?"

Mia's face crumpled as she tried once again to pull away from Josiah's grip. "Oh no, you're wrong. I would never try to hurt Zoey. She is our leader. We couldn't have survived out here without her."

"Crying won't help," Zoey replied, her voice firm. She appeared unaffected by Mia's tears. "My guess is, you were hoping if I was killed on the first day, the boat would immediately come back and get you all. But you were wrong. Once you found out we were stuck out here, you and Lucas decided you needed me to guide you back to the base camp, so then you killed the others on your list."

Josiah glanced around the campground. He noticed a tree that met his needs and led Mia over to it as Zoey lit their way with the flashlight.

"I'm innocent," Mia declared as she dragged her feet, still pulling against Josiah's grip. "I've never hurt anyone."

"I think Lucas would disagree." Zoey shook her head. "When Janey got hurt, you suddenly had the perfect opportunity to take his life."

"Lucas is the one who killed Marty Garcia and Patricia. I had nothing to do with it."

"Then why steal the notebook?" Zoey asked.

"I was afraid there might be something in it that would hurt Lucas's memory," Mia responded lamely.

"Save it for your court hearing," Josiah replied tersely. "I hope you've enjoyed your last few days of freedom. I imagine you'll be in prison for the rest of your life."

Josiah pulled a rope out of his pocket and tied Mia, sitting down, to the Aspen tree he'd selected. He stretched her hands behind her back and tied them securely so she couldn't reach the knot. He didn't want to take a chance of her escaping anytime during the rest of the night. When he was finished, he took back the flashlight and once again shone it on Mia. Within seconds, her face lost its innocent mask and contorted with rage. Evidently, she realized she wasn't going to convince them of her virtue. Bitterness seemed to seep from every pore of her body.

"You'll never prove a thing," she said viciously.

"Well, now that's where you're wrong," Josiah said. "We have John Webster, who will testify how Marty Garcia was embezzling funds from Western, and how Patricia discovered what was going on and saved copies of everything. Webster is willing to admit his own part of the scheme and will probably make some sort of plea deal."

"How did you know about Patricia's blackmail?" Mia suddenly asked. "Could you read the shorthand after all?"

Josiah smiled. "Actually, we didn't know about the blackmail for sure until you just admitted it. It was just conjecture on our part," he replied.

"Once we have this notebook translated," Zoey said confidently as she waved it in front of Mia, "I'm sure we'll discover even more. This little book will be a treasure trove of information once we get it into law enforcement's hands. No doubt it will confirm the motives for Lucas's murders, and yours as well." She zipped the book safely in her jacket pocket and Mia actually stomped her foot in frustration and kicked leaves at Zoey as she twisted against the ropes that secured her hands.

"Patricia was a gossip and a liar. She made all sorts of baseless accusations, when the truth is, that woman was a criminal in her own right. That book proves nothing besides her own guilt in this whole mess."

Zoey shrugged. "Maybe. But your actions tell another story. Otherwise, why would you try to get the book away from me tonight? This notebook has you scared. I'm sure Detective Lockhart will find the contents very enlightening."

"And we have the anchor that you used to kill Lucas with," Josiah added. "We're turning it over to the police tomorrow, too. I bet forensics will discover your fingerprints on the shank."

Mia's eyes flashed, but she finally drew her lips together and said nothing further.

Josiah checked the knots once again. Confident that Mia couldn't escape, he took Zoey's hand and led her away from Mia so they could talk without the bound woman eavesdropping. Once they were out of Mia's sight and hearing distance but still had enough firelight to see each other, he pulled her into an embrace and held her tightly for a moment, relishing her warmth and the knowledge that she was safe. Relief swept over him in waves. After a few moments, he finally pulled back and met her eyes. "Good plan, Zoey. It worked like a charm." He gave her a smile, then leaned forward and gave her a quick kiss on the lips. "Get some rest. I'll take first watch, and Rick knows to come relieve me at 2:00 a.m." He released her and she stepped back, a soft pink barely visible on her cheeks.

"Sounds like a deal." She returned his smile. "We make a good team."

"We certainly do," Josiah said. He leaned over and kissed her gently on the lips a second time, finally confident that they were safe. Finally, the killers had been stopped.

The next morning, Zoey spent quite a bit of time on the radio talking to Detective Lockhart. His law enforcement office had confirmed that Western was suffering financially and was about to declare bankruptcy. When Josiah's father, Chase Quinn, had sold his shares and left the company, it had basically spelled the beginning of the end for the entire business, and Garcia's embezzlement had been the proverbial nail in the coffin. Lucas had given his life to Western, and rather than see it fail as a result of Garcia's and Chase's actions, he had tried to save the company and had even used his own money to try to fill the holes. Unfortunately, he had not been able to undo the damage. It was just too little, too late, and Western's fate was sealed.

That insight helped but still didn't explain all of the deaths or Mia's actions. Zoey and Josiah took some breakfast over to Mia, whose hands were still tied tightly behind her back. Although Josiah stood within hearing distance, at Zoey's request he stayed back so Mia would focus on her. The woman seemed to really hate Josiah, probably because he had been the one to physically foil her plans, but Zoey was hoping somehow she could get the woman talking.

"Are you hungry?" Zoey asked.

There was no way Zoey was going to release Mia, but she was willing to spoon-feed her if the woman wanted breakfast. She offered Mia a bowl of oatmeal, and when she nodded, Zoey offered her a bite, hoping that she could get some information that would answer the dozens of questions that were still floating around in her head.

"So, I don't understand why you tried to drown me on the first day of the trip."

"Who said I did?" Mia said between bites.

"Looking back now, it's obvious. And since you're going to prison anyway, why not come clean? I still don't understand why you would want to hurt me. I didn't even know you or Lucas before this trip. Why would you want to kill me?"

Mia tilted her head but finally answered. Apparently, she realized her fate was sealed and nothing could stop her from going to prison. That understanding finally loosened her tongue. "Chase Quinn destroyed Western when he pulled out his money. We had several large contracts for supplies and tech support that were eliminated when the customers found out what Chase had done, and once that happened, other contracts started disappearing as well. Do you know how many people work for Western, or how long Lucas and I have been involved with that company? Do you know we sacrificed to make it a success? We were the backbone of the business, and Lucas was one of the original employees that started it all twenty-seven years ago. Chase Quinn destroyed our livelihood, and I wanted to annihilate Tikaani to pay him back for destroying Western. It's as simple as that. I know he had other businesses, but this company is the one he loved. It was obvious, especially with the way he always tried to get Western's employees to take expeditions as team-building exercises. I wanted Chase to get a taste of his own medicine." She shrugged. "You already had a customer complaint, which I orchestrated, by the way, so I thought I'd just add fuel to the fire by having you get hurt or killed right at the beginning of the trip. If word got out that Tikaani's main guide was incompetent, then everyone would cancel their reservations, and Tikaani would eventually fold."

Zoey thought back to all the stress and heartache that complaint had caused, and how close she had come to drowning in the bay, yet Mia spoke about it as if ruining someone's reputation and hurting or killing someone were par for the course. Despite her hurt and frustration, Zoey tried to move on. "Okay, that explains your attack on me, but what about the other deaths? Why try to hurt Josiah?"

Mia squinted her eyes. "When Lucas realized we couldn't get the boat back and we needed you to guide us, he decided to take his revenge on Josiah. Killing him would destroy Tikaani just as well, or if it didn't, then he would have killed Chase's son, which was just as satisfying." She accepted another bite of food and swallowed, a serene smile on her face that to Zoey was even scarier than the look she'd had when she'd been wielding the knife. "Marty Garcia was embezzling funds. Everybody knows that now. His actions caused Western to struggle even more. Lucas might have had a chance to turn it around after Chase left if Garcia hadn't been so greedy. But Garcia did so much damage, there was no way to recover."

"And Patricia?" Zoey prompted, offering another bite of food.

"Patricia confronted Lucas during the trip. She tried to blackmail him since he had covered up Garcia's corruption. She claimed she had dozens of emails and business documents, and if we didn't pay her, she was going to reveal everything to law enforcement at the end of this trip." She gritted her teeth. "That woman never did understand. Lucas was trying to do everything he could to save the company, but she just wanted to destroy it, just like Garcia."

Josiah approached and spoke to Mia. "Then why kill Lucas?" he asked, confusion painting his features. "It sounds like he cared about Western and was doing everything he could to save it. He even killed for the company."

Mia kicked aimlessly at the dirt with her boot but finally answered. "Lucas started out on the right track, but before I knew it, he had mortgaged everything we owned to the hilt, and had put our last dollar into the business. Because of his actions, we're going to lose more than just our jobs when Western declares bankruptcy. We'll lose our house, our cars and everything else we own." She squinted up at Josiah and drew her lips into a thin line in a slow, deliberate motion. "I was poor growing up, and I hated every day of it. There was no way I was going to lose everything just because Lucas loved Western more than he loved me."

Zoey felt sick to her stomach. How could someone live with so much hatred and bitterness inside of them? She shared Mia's frustration with Chase's and Garcia's actions that had hurt so many people, but how could murder ever be the answer?

NINETEEN

Josiah watched pensively as Detective Lockhart hand-cuffed Mia and led her over to another officer, who escorted her to the waiting law enforcement boat that was docked at the river's mouth. Instead of a defeated posture, Mia walked almost proudly, her spine erect, as she left the group behind her. Her behavior left a bitter taste in his mouth. He had started this trip wanting to emulate his father and learn how to replicate his business practices that had created such an amazing portfolio of success. Now he knew that copying the man's behavior was the last thing he'd ever want to do. Chase Quinn may have looked successful on the balance sheets, but his methods had hurt dozens, if not hundreds, of people, and because of his father's selfishness and failure to report the problems he'd discovered at Western, a thriving business had failed. Granted, there were other contributing factors, such as the embezzlement that had come to light soon after. Chase's behavior might not have been criminal, but it was surely immoral. If Chase had tried to fix the problems instead of pulling out his money and abandoning the company, Western just might have been saved, as well as the jobs of the people who depended upon Western for their livelihoods.

Josiah unzipped his jacket and removed Patricia's notebook. He may not know a lot about business, but he did know a lot about people. He had learned several life lessons during his command in the army, and with Christ as his guidepost, he was determined from this day forward to make his inheritance his own. Instead of trying to maintain the status quo, or follow in his father's footsteps, Josiah wanted to make sure each company was being run ethically and benefited the employees as well as the customers. He already had some ideas for how he could accomplish that and was eager to talk to the management teams at the various companies he now owned and get their input as well. One thing he was sure of—profit alone would no longer be the measurement of success for the Quinn family portfolio.

He turned to Detective Lockhart and handed him the notebook. "This belonged to Patricia, who worked in Western's accounting department. She claimed to have evidence of the embezzlement and other things happening at the company. If you get the shorthand translated in this notebook, I think you'll see that she was trying to blackmail Lucas Phillips regarding some embezzlement and other problems that were occurring in their company. We found this among her belongings after she died. I'd also check her hard drives at work and home, in case her claims were true, and she has copies of the documents you need to prove the embezzlement."

Lockhart took the book and thumbed through it, then secured it in his own pocket. "Thanks. Our stenographer will make short work of this once I get it back to the office."

The two men glanced over at the weary Tikaani group of campers who had arrived at Nuka an hour or so ago, and who were now storing the kayaks and organizing their belongings and equipment. Relief was evident on everyone's faces that the trip had finally come to an end and they would soon be taxied back to the base camp.

After a few minutes, Zoey broke away from her leadership duties and approached Josiah and Detective Lockhart. Introductions were made as she shook hands with the officer. "Everyone's squared away. Tikaani's boat is down by the law enforcement boat, and we'll be ready to go whenever you say the word, Detective."

"That's good to hear," Lockhart confirmed. "Once we're back at the base camp, we'll organize interviews, but we want to get everyone back to town first and let them relax a bit. I'm sure this trip has been a harrowing experience."

Zoey nodded in agreement. Then she opened her backpack and handed the officer the knife that had killed Marty Garcia, as well as the bloody kayak anchor that had been used to bludgeon Lucas. Each was wrapped separately in a sealed plastic bag. "You'll want these, too. Just let us know if you need anything further from us. We'll help you in any way we can."

"Will do," Lockhart confirmed as he shook both of their hands again. "Thanks for all of your help with this case. We have Mia Phillips secured and will be leaving momentarily. All I ask is that you let us get out of your way before you take Tikaani's boat out."

"No problem," Josiah agreed. "I know you were investigating this case ever since we reported the first murder via the radio and that you've learned a lot just in the last few days. Have you discovered anything new since we talked yesterday? Mia's motive still seems a bit sketchy."

Lockhart nodded. "We've done a deep dive into Mia and Lucas Phillips' finances and lifestyle. We've also interviewed several close friends and family members, who gave us some invaluable insight into their relationship. Apparently, Mia Phillips is all about appearances. When she found out Lucas had put all their money into the company and they were going to lose everything, she was furious. She would no longer be able to keep up financially with her friends, and the anger and frustration have been slowly growing into an inferno over the last few months. If she hadn't been caught, Mia would have received a two-million-dollar life insurance policy upon Lucas's death. It looks like she killed him to get that money and maintain her lavish lifestyle."

"So it all boils down to money," Zoe said with a bitter tone.

"Unfortunately, it sure looks that way," Lockhart said. He touched the brim of his hat. "You two take care and travel safely back to your home base. I'll be in touch."

Josiah nodded. "Thank you, Detective. We sure appreciate your time and effort."

The two watched him go back to the shore and get

into the boat where Mia sat stiffly, her handcuffs securing her to a ring by her seat. Two other officers were also in the boat, and they launched and left as soon as Lockhart was settled at the steering wheel.

Zoey turned to Josiah. "You look concerned. Care to share?"

He reached over and slowly took her hand, then interlocked their fingers. The rest of the group was out of hearing distance, but he lowered his voice anyway. "I'm just thinking through everything that has happened during this trip. My father's actions caused so much trouble and heartache. If he had done the right thing back at the beginning, maybe nobody would have died or even gotten hurt on this trip."

"True, but he's not the only one to blame. The embezzlement would have destroyed the company eventually, and we don't know that Chase would have been able to fix the damage even if he had stayed. When he pulled out his money, he just made the house of cards start to collapse a little sooner than it might have otherwise."

Josiah lightly squeezed her hand. "I agree, but I've made some decisions. The biggest is that from now on, I want Christ to be at the center of all my decisions. I've been praying about this a lot. I have some work to do to become familiar with all my new responsibilities, but I've decided to run the companies as God leads, rather than trying to follow in my father's footsteps. I think I had almost idolized him, but he was just a man, and an imperfect one at that."

Zoey smiled. "Aren't we all? We all make mistakes. And don't forget, Chase had his good qualities as well.

He helped me get my life back on track and regain my confidence. For that I'll always be grateful." She looked up into Josiah's eyes. "But putting Jesus first is a lesson I've learned this trip as well. I keep trying to do things on my own and then wonder why I struggle when it all starts to fall apart. This trip has been a great reminder about what is really important in life, and how I also need to make sure Jesus is at the center of all I do." She took her free hand and gently drew her fingers down his cheek. "I'm so relieved that the killer has finally been apprehended. I feel like I can relax for the first time since we started this trip." She let her hand fall. "So, what's next for you?"

Josiah smiled and took her other hand so he was now holding both of them and turned her gently to face him. "Well, I'd like to take a break for a few days and recover from all of this, but then I think we should start planning the next expedition. I'm pretty sure we'll still have some reservations after all the dust settles, but even if it takes a while to spring back after all of this, I want to make Tikaani a success again. You're still my leader and guide, and you will still be in charge like before, but if you're willing, I'd like to accompany you sometimes and do it as a team. I'd like to take this trip again without the violence and just enjoy the scenery."

She smiled at him, apparently catching the double meaning of his words. "I'd like that, Josiah. I think we make a pretty good team."

He moved closer and leaned forward to rest his forehead against hers. "We do indeed. You know, after my last relationship crashed and burned, I was afraid to trust anyone ever again with my heart. But I trust you, Zoey. I am offering you my heart, right here and now. If you're willing, I'd like to get to know you better and see where this relationship goes." He tilted his head and gave her a gentle kiss on the lips. They were so soft! "I love you, Zoey." He released her hands and gently cupped her cheeks with his hands as the kiss lingered. Electricity shot down his arms and legs as the attraction sparked between them.

The kiss finally ended, and he pulled her into his embrace and just enjoyed the closeness. She was warm and soft, and a happiness enveloped him that he thought he would never feel again. God had restored and strengthened their relationship with Him and had brought him a beautiful woman to share the future with. As a result, the path for his life that had once terrified him now left him filled with excitement.

Zoey enjoyed the embrace. Could this really be happening to her? Could this man who was holding her truly love her the way she loved him? When Josiah had arrived for the expedition, she had been terrified of him and his plans for Tikaani and her future. Now not only was her job secure, but God had also used Josiah to help her work through her insecurities and relationship doubts. She was ready to trust again, and she was convinced that God had given her a second chance. "I'll take it!" she said playfully and gave him a gentle squeeze. "And I offer you my heart in return." She smiled and said a silent prayer.

Thank You, Lord, for bringing this wonderful man into my life. With Your help, I'm convinced we can handle our future together, no matter where it leads. I am so blessed!

* * * * *

*If you liked this story from Kathleen Tailer,
check out her previous
Love Inspired Suspense books.*

Covert Takedown
Held for Ransom
Everglades Escape
Deadly Cover-Up
Perilous Pursuit
Undercover Jeopardy
Quest for Justice
Perilous Refuge
The Reluctant Witness
Under the Marshal's Protection

*Available now from Love Inspired Suspense!
Find more great reads at www.LoveInspired.com.*

Dear Reader,

I got the opportunity to travel to Alaska a couple of years ago and was just amazed at the majestic mountains and beauty I saw in every direction. God has now allowed me to travel to all fifty states and to twenty-four countries, and I am totally awed by His creation and, more importantly, by all of the wonderful and inspiring people I have met along the way. If you enjoy traveling, I encourage you to start planning your next trip now. Does your church do mission work in other states or countries? Do you love giving, learning, and sharing your faith? If you are new to traveling and love people, joining a mission team is an excellent way to get started.

Please visit my website, www.kathleentailer.com, and my Facebook page, www.Facebook.com/ktailer to learn more about the mission work going on in Africa.

May God bless you!
Kathleen Tailer

HARLEQUIN
PLUS

Try the best multimedia subscription service for romance readers like you!

Read, Watch and Play.

Experience the easiest way to get the romance content you crave.

Start your **FREE TRIAL** at
<u>www.harlequinplus.com/freetrial</u>.